Frosted Secrets

Frosted Secrets

Hannah R Hunt

1

The morning sun streamed through the sheer curtains, casting a golden light over the modest bedroom. Miranda lay still for a moment, listening to the rhythmic breathing of Nick beside her, his warmth radiating beneath the covers. Tinsel, their tabby cat, lay curled at their feet, her tail flicking lazily as if sensing that morning had arrived far too soon.

Miranda shifted slightly, and immediately Tinsel's ears twitched, her golden eyes opening halfway to fix a watchful gaze on her. Miranda smiled softly, noticing how Tinsel seemed particularly attuned to her lately—always alert, always close.

With a soft sigh, Miranda turned onto her side, propping herself up on one elbow as she watched Nick sleep. His brow relaxed, his expression at peace, and for a fleeting moment, she wished she could freeze time.

"I can feel you staring at me," Nick muttered, voice thick with sleep.

Miranda grinned. "Well, you're not wrong."

His lips curled into a lazy smile before he cracked one eye open. "If you're up, then that means coffee should be involved."

She nudged him playfully. "Maybe I was just admiring my husband. Ever think of that?"

Nick groaned dramatically, stretching his arms over his head before pulling the blankets tighter around himself. "Mm. Flattery's nice, but I still think coffee would be nicer."

Miranda laughed as she threw off the covers and padded toward the kitchen, Tinsel immediately hopping down to follow her. The cat wove affectionately between her feet, rubbing her head against

Miranda's ankles with a purposeful insistence as she set about making coffee.

"You're just as bad as him," Miranda murmured fondly, scooping kibble into Tinsel's bowl before pouring fresh water alongside it. Tinsel purred in satisfaction before digging in, the morning light catching a small, delicate snowflake-shaped marking on her back hip—a detail Miranda had always admired but rarely thought deeply about.

By the time Nick joined her in the kitchen, still mussed from sleep but looking effortlessly handsome, the coffee was ready. He kissed her on the cheek as he reached past her for a mug. "What would I do without you?"

She let a knowing grin curve her lips over the rim of her cup. "Drink terrible gas station coffee and forget to feed the cat."

Nick took a slow sip before conceding, "Fair point."

Tinsel leaped onto the table, breaking the moment as she wove between their coffee cups, searching for attention. Nick chuckled, scratching behind her ears. "Guess she's making sure we don't get too sentimental."

Miranda shook her head, smiling. "She's just making sure everything is okay."

After breakfast, Nick grabbed Tinsel and held her up like a trophy. "Alright, little troublemaker, time for your morning zoomies?"

Tinsel flicked her tail in response, wriggling out of his arms to settle next to Miranda instead, her gaze watchful, protective. Nick dramatically sighed. "She never cuddles with me willingly."

"That's because she knows you're the one who moves too much in bed," Miranda teased, rinsing out her coffee mug. "I, on the other hand, am a cat-approved human."

Nick scoffed. "That just means she thinks she owns you."

"And?" Miranda shot him a playful look. "She does."

Tinsel, satisfied everything was well, suddenly streaked past them, skidding to a halt near her scratching post before pouncing onto it with a victorious chirp. Nick shook his head, a reluctant smile tugging at his lips. "Yep. We live under feline rule."

She swatted him lightly as she headed toward the bedroom to get dressed. "Come on, or we'll be late."

Nick followed, feigning exasperation. "You say that like you don't take fifteen minutes just to pick out socks."

"Excuse me, but sock choices matter," she countered, throwing a pair at him. He caught them effortlessly.

They continued their back and forth while getting ready, moving in sync through their shared space. It was a morning like any other—comforting, full of routine, and sprinkled with the laughter that had always come so easily between them.

Nick teased Miranda about how long it took her to find the right sweater, she retaliated by hiding his keys for a full two minutes, and they danced around each other in the small bathroom, brushing their teeth in playful sync.

Before heading out, Nick grabbed his coat and leaned in, pressing a kiss to Miranda's forehead. "Be good today."

She arched her brow. "That's more of a challenge than you think."

He chuckled. "I know. That's why I said it."

On the drive to her client's house, Miranda propped her feet up on the dashboard as Nick navigated the quiet roads. She had a prenatal home visit scheduled that morning—one of her favorite parts of being a midwife. There was something sacred about stepping into a family's space, bringing reassurance right to their doorstep.

The warmth of September drifted through the open window, golden and crisp, carrying the faint scent of fallen leaves and woodsmoke. But even now, patches of snow clung stubbornly to the edges of the forest floor. In Fir Hollow, the seasons shifted, but the snow never seemed to fully disappear.

"You know that's illegal, right?" he teased, nodding toward her feet.

"What, my unmatched ability to make the perfect morning playlist?"

"No, putting your feet up like that. If I crash, your knees will end up in your eyeballs."

She made a dramatic gasp. "Are you planning to crash? Because if so, I'd like to get out now."

Nick rolled his eyes. "I'm just saying—"

"Oh, here we go. Nick's famous Safety Lectures. Shall I take notes?"

"Forget it," he said, shaking his head with a chuckle. "Just don't sue me when your legs fold like a pretzel."

"You're assuming I'd survive to sue you."

"You would. You're too much of a stubborn redhead to not to."

Her mouth curved in quiet agreement. "That's probably true."

They pulled up to her client's house, and Nick put the SUV in park. "Text me when you're done."

"Yes, dad."

"Miranda—"

She leaned over and kissed his cheek. "I'm kidding. I will."

As she stepped out, Nick called after her, "Hey, what happened to 'admiring your husband' this morning?"

She shot a wink. "Still admiring. Just in a different way now."

With a laugh, she closed the door and walked up the path. Miranda paused at the doorstep, a sudden chill brushing her neck despite the sun's warmth. Goosebumps prickled along her arms.

A ridiculous reaction, surely. Maybe the wind had just shifted.

Still, she hesitated for half a second before stepping inside. *Lord, keep me safe,* she thought, the simple prayer slipping through her mind like second nature. Then, shaking off the strange unease, she reached for the doorknob and stepped forward.

2

As Miranda disappeared through the front door of her client's home, Nick lingered a moment, watching her go before pulling away. Even after all these years, she still amazed him. It wasn't just her skill or knowledge—it was the way she truly saw people, made them feel valued. Whether it was a nervous first-time mother or a weary grandmother who had seen it all, Miranda had a way of meeting people exactly where they were.

She gave them her full attention, her whole heart. And that was one of the many reasons he loved her.

With a soft chuckle, he shook his head and pulled away from the curb. He had a whole hour to himself before he needed to pick her up—an unexpected bit of freedom. The roads were clear, the crisp morning air carried a hint of lingering frost, and the car felt good beneath his hands. A little joyride wouldn't hurt.

The thought alone sent a ripple of excitement through him. It had been too long since he'd simply driven for the pleasure of it, letting the open road stretch before him with no destination in mind.

As he merged onto the highway, he rolled the window down slightly, letting the cold air bite at his skin. The hum of the engine beneath him, the steady rhythm of the tires against the pavement—it was a kind of freedom he hadn't realized he'd missed.

He let himself settle into the drive, one hand resting loosely on the wheel. The town gave way to rolling countryside, frost-dusted fields stretching wide beneath a pale blue sky. Sunlight glinted off the icy patches that clung stubbornly to the edges of the road.

Nick adjusted the radio, flipping past static and talk shows until he landed on an old rock station. The familiar guitar riff lit something in him—he tapped the steering wheel in time, lips quirking upward in quiet appreciation.

A good song. A good drive. A good morning.

For the first time in a while, he felt... light.

Not that life had been bad—far from it. But things had felt heavier lately. Miranda seemed to have clients back to back, he was busy building custom furniture, and sometimes the weight of responsibility had a way of pressing down before you even realized it.

Maybe that's why this small moment of freedom felt so good.

A memory tugged at him. Miranda would shake her head if she saw him like this. He could almost hear her voice, playful but firm: *Don't push your luck, Nick.*

A smirk played at the corner of his lips. Just a little longer.

One stretch of Route 14 always stayed cold, tucked beneath the evergreens where sunlight barely reached. Snowmelt from the night before had frozen into a near-invisible glaze across the asphalt—a lingering quirk of Fir Hollow, where summer warmth never quite melted everything away.

The road curved ahead, the morning light shimmering over the asphalt. Everything felt perfect—the kind of peace that settled into your bones and made you forget that life had any sharp edges at all.

He never saw it coming.

One moment, the tires gripped the pavement with steady confidence. The next—nothing.

The car hit black ice.

His stomach lurched as the back end fishtailed, the vehicle twisting violently against his control. His hands clenched the wheel, but it was useless—the car had its own mind now. A helpless, weightless kind of panic gripped him.

Turn into the skid.

He tried. It didn't matter.

The world outside became a blur—trees, sky, pavement, spinning together in a dizzying spiral. The tires screeched in protest, the sound clawing at his ears. His breath came in sharp bursts, his pulse a frantic drumbeat against his ribs.

Lord! Help me!

The impact came too fast to brace for.

A sickening crunch of metal.

His body was thrown sideways as the passenger side slammed into a tree, the force rattling through him like a lightning strike. His skull struck the window—a burst of pain so sharp, so blinding, it stole the air from his lungs. Glass shattered around him, stinging his skin. The seatbelt wrenched him back, digging into his ribs like a vice.

For a second, everything was noise. The hiss of steam curling from the mangled hood.

Through the shattered windshield, Nick caught a blurry glimpse of a semi parked on the shoulder of the road, just beyond the bend. He couldn't tell if it had just arrived or had been sitting there the whole time.

My phone.

He fumbled weakly, but his limbs felt distant, disconnected from him. His vision blurred at the edges. The world narrowed.

Then—

Nothing.

Static crackled over the radio.

"Male driver, unconscious. Severe head trauma. Possible internal injuries."

Boots crunched against the icy pavement as first responders swarmed the wreck. Flashing red and blue lights cut through the pale morning fog, reflecting off the shattered glass that littered the ground.

"Pulse is weak but present."

"Get that door open—now!"

Metal groaned as they pried the twisted frame, working against time. The car had folded inward from the impact, trapping the driver inside. Blood streaked the dashboard, a stark contrast to the frost-covered windshield.

"Sir, can you hear me?"

No response.

One of the paramedics leaned closer, pressing two fingers against Nick's throat. "He's still with us." He turned towards the others. "We need to move fast."

A few feet away, a man stood near the roadside, hands shoved into his coat pockets, his breath curling in the cold morning air.

He hadn't meant to be here.

Not like this.

His car had been a few yards behind when it happened—one second, the road had been clear, and the next, the vehicle ahead of him had spun out of control. He had barely registered the skid before the impact sent the car crashing into the tree, metal crumpling like paper.

For a moment, all he had done was sit there, gripping the wheel, staring.

Now, as he watched first responders work, something in his chest tightened.

He recognized the man in the driver's seat.

A cold weight settled in his stomach. He took an unconscious step back, his heart hammering in his chest.

It's him.

Of all the people. Of all the places.

His fingers curled into fists as he took another step away, glancing toward the flashing lights, the chaos of the rescue scene. They wouldn't notice him. Not now.

But still—he lingered.

Not because he cared.

But because this... this was unexpected.

A slow exhale left his lips as he took one last look at the man they were pulling from the wreck.

Then, without a word, he turned, got back in his car, and drove away.

3

Everything was quiet.

Until the ambulance skidded to a halt outside the ER entrance, shattering the fragile peace with a rush of paramedics and a flurry of urgent voices.

The back doors burst open, and paramedics swiftly pulled Nick's stretcher onto the pavement.

"He's unresponsive. Head Trauma. BP dropping," one called out as they rushed him inside.

The hospital doors swung open, flooding the stretcher with harsh fluorescent light. A flurry of scrubs and hurried footsteps surrounded them. The scent of antiseptic stung the air. Nurses and doctors moved with precision, barely pausing as they took in the unconscious man before them.

"Pupils sluggish. Possible brain swelling. We need a CT scan now," another voice cut in, firm and urgent.

Nick's body remained completely still as they transferred him to a hospital bed, hands moving rapidly to hook him up to IV's and monitors. The rapid beep of a heart monitor filled the space, a stark contrast to the heavy silence of his motionless body.

"Prep him for intubation," a doctor ordered. "He needs to be stabilized."

There was no reaction, no flicker of awareness. Nick was gone to the world, submerged in unconsciousness as machines took over the fight for him. His body moved only at the hands of the doctors and nurses working over him, but he felt none of it, saw none of it.

They wheeled him out of the trauma room toward radiology, his still form lost beneath a tangle of wires and tubes.

Hours passed in the void. Once the CT scan was complete, they wheeled him into the ICU, his body carefully monitored for any changes. Machines beeped in steady rhythm, keeping track of his vitals as a team of doctors worked over him.

The sharp scent of antiseptic crept into his awareness.

A faint, rhythmic beeping. Voices—some hushed, others clinical and detached—moved around him. The air was cold. Too cold.

Where's Miranda?

Nick tried to open his eyes, but his body wouldn't obey. Panic clawed its way through his chest. He tried again—moving, speaking, anything—but he was trapped, his mind fully awake while his body refused to respond.

Machines hummed around him. A heavy weight pressed against his face and throat. A breathing tube.

I need my wife! Why can't anybody hear me?

He felt weightless, disconnected—floating just beneath the surface of awareness, tethered to the world only by the sounds around him.

Somewhere, deep in the fog, a memory stirred.

Laughter.

He could hear Miranda's voice, light and teasing. *"You have to let me win at least once, Nick."* A memory of them at the lake, skipping rocks, her playful pout when his stone bounced four times while hers sank instantly. Sunlight kissed her hair, turning it golden, her eyes full of warmth. He could feel the water lapping at his ankles, the cool breeze against his skin.

Another flicker of memory—her hand on his chest, her lips brushing his cheek before she whispered, *"Come back to me."*

The memory slipped through his grasp like sand.

I need to wake up!

Dr. Winters, his voice low and measured: "Vitals are stable, but I'm concerned about head trauma. What were the results of the CT scan?"

A nurse adjusted his IV drip. "Mild concussion, severe swelling, but no fractures."

Dr. Winters studied the images. "The best thing for him right now is rest. Let's put him into a medically induced coma and give his brain the opportunity to rest. Waking up too soon could be fatal."

No!

No, don't put me under! I need to wake up!

Nick wanted to scream, to force his limbs to move, but he remained paralyzed in the prison of his own body.

Then—a name.

Miranda.

His heart surged at the sound. He knew that name. It was his anchor, his tether to the world. The nurse's voice was distant, but real.

"His wife's name is Miranda," the nurse murmured, passing a small slip of paper. "Here's her number."

Nick fought against the weight of his body, against the darkness trying to pull him under.

I'm here! Miranda, I'm here!

Dr. Winters then turned his attention to the monitors. "His blood pressure is still low, but he seems to be responding well to the fluids. Keep monitoring his intracranial pressure closely. I'll notify his wife of his condition."

"Don't put me out! I need my wife!" The thought rang in his mind, desperate and raw. But no one heard. No one could.

As the sedatives seeped into his system, his thoughts became sluggish. The world slipped further away.

The laughter, the touch, the memories of Miranda faded into nothing.

And then, there was only silence.

Across town, in the warmth of her client's cozy living room, Miranda felt an unexplained chill ripple through her chest, as though something vital had suddenly happened.

4

Miranda adjusted the strap of her bag as she stepped onto the wraparound porch of the Johnsons' home, inhaling the crisp morning air. A faint scent of pine lingered, carried by the gentle breeze that rustled through the trees lining the property. The house, a cozy two-story with white siding and dark green shutters, exuded warmth, even from the outside. She knocked softly, mindful of the possibility that the mother-to-be might still be resting.

As she waited, a strange prickle crawled up the back of her neck, subtle but insistent. The air felt different—just a fraction cooler than it had moments ago, as if a shadow had passed through the morning light. She glanced toward the trees, frowning slightly. The branches swayed lazily in the breeze, the forest quiet aside from the occasional chirp of a bird. Normal. Nothing out of place.

Still, her fingers tightened slightly on the strap of her bag. She had the sudden, ridiculous urge to turn around, to scan the street, the treeline, the spaces in between. But she didn't.

The door creaked open, revealing Julia Johnson, a young woman in her late twenties with kind eyes and a hand resting protectively over her rounded belly. "Miranda! Come in. I just made some tea. Would you like some?"

"That sounds wonderful, thank you," Miranda said with a smile, stepping inside.

My imagination is running wild. That must have been the morning chill.

The interior was bathed in soft morning light filtering through the sheer curtains. The scent of chamomile tea mingled with the faint aroma of freshly baked bread, creating a sense of comfort and home.

They settled in the living room, where Julia eased herself onto the couch with a slight groan. Miranda took the seat across from her, pulling out her notebook. "How have you been feeling? Any new discomforts since our last visit?"

Julia sighed, rubbing slow circles over her belly. "Just the usual—achy back, some trouble sleeping. The baby's been extra active at night."

Miranda nodded knowingly. "That's common at this stage. It's like they're having their own little dance party when you're trying to rest. Have you been doing the stretches I showed you?"

"Yes, and they help. A little, at least." Julia chuckled softly before taking a sip of tea. "I think I'm just getting impatient. It feels like I've been pregnant forever."

Miranda smiled reassuringly. "You're in the home stretch now. The last few weeks can feel the longest, but your body is doing exactly what it needs to. Have you thought more about your birth plan? Any changes since we last talked?"

Julia hesitated, biting her lip. "I still want a home birth, but my mom keeps telling me I should be in a hospital, just in case. It's making me second-guess myself."

"It's natural to have doubts, especially with so many opinions coming at you," Miranda said gently. "But this is your birth, your choice. I'm here to make sure you feel confident and safe, whatever you decide. We'll go over the plan again, talk through any concerns, and make sure you have all the information you need."

Julia exhaled, some of the tension in her shoulders easing. "That would really help. I just want to do what's best for the baby."

"And you are," Miranda assured her. "I tell every mother that I help to trust their instincts. They always know the right answer.

Now. Let's go over some relaxation techniques that may help with the sleepless nights. As long as the baby cooperates."

They spent the next thirty minutes reviewing breathing exercises and comfort measures, Julia gradually growing more at ease. As Miranda packed up, she glanced at the clock. "Nick should be back soon to pick me up. I want you to try the warm compress on your lower back tonight and let me know how it feels. If that doesn't seem to help I've got a chiropractor friend that does prenatal alignments."

"I will. Thanks again, Miranda. You always make me feel better after our visits."

She gathered her bag and slipped her arms through the straps, but as she straightened, a sudden chill crept over her skin. The warmth of the cozy home flickered—just for a second—like the flame of a candle caught in an unseen draft. A dull, distant sensation thrummed through her chest, a whisper of something colliding, something breaking.

As quickly as it started, it stopped.

Miranda blinked.

What was that? That was weird! I've never felt that before.

A trick of the nerves, maybe.

Shaking off the strange unease, she gave Julia one last smile and headed for the door. "I'll see you next week. Or sooner if the baby decides it's time."

Outside, the bitter air stung her cheeks. The clouds hung low and gray. She pulled her coat tighter, expecting to see Nick's car waiting at the curb.

But the street was empty.

Pulling her phone from her pocket she saw no missed calls. Not even a text message. She quickly dialed Nick's number, but the call went straight to voicemail.

"Hey, it's Nicholas Owens. Leave a message, and I'll get back to you as soon as I can."

Miranda's heart skipped a beat, and she ended the call, her fingers lingering over the screen as tightness settled in her chest.

Did he get caught up? Lose track of time? Or... is something wrong?

The thought whispered through her mind, cold and unwanted. She shook it off.

Nick is fine. He's enjoying his joyride.

Still, frustration prickled at the edges of her patience. With a sigh, she adjusted her bag and started walking. It wasn't too far from home. Just a couple of miles.

And besides, it wasn't her first time she'd been left to find her way home.

Nick and cars!

Making her way down the road, the uneasy feeling from earlier crept back, a ghost of something she couldn't quite place.

By the time she reached the cottage, her fingers were stiff from the cold. Snow still clung to the ground around their house, as it always did—no matter the season.

She stomped the snow from her boots and pushed the door open, the warmth of home wrapping around her. Just as she shrugged off her coat, her cell phone rang. It's jolly jingle echoing through the quiet.

Pulling her phone out of her purse, she frowned at the unrecognized number on the screen.

A feeling of unease washed over her again.

Shaking it off as nothing, she answers the phone. "Hello?"

"Is this Mrs. Owens?" says a male voice.

"This is she. May I ask who's calling?" she says as she scrapes the remaining snow off of her boots. Miranda pressed the phone tighter against her ear.

"Mrs. Owens, this is Dr. Winters from Trinity Hospital. Your husband has been in an accident—"

5

The world tilted.

No.

No, that didn't make sense. Nick was fine this morning. He was supposed to pick her up in an hour. This was just a misunderstanding.

She blinked, her grip tightening on the doorframe for balance.

"Are you still there ma'am?"

The words finally registered. A lead weight settled deep in her chest.

Nick. Accident. Hospital

This is real.

Her heart slammed against her ribs. The room blurred around her as the floor seemed to disappear beneath her feet.

"Is he—?" Her voice cracked.

"He's alive," the doctor reassured her quickly. "But unconscious. We're running tests now. You should come as soon as possible."

The phone nearly slipped from her fingers.

"I'm... on my way."

Miranda wiped at her face, barely realizing she was crying. Scrambling to her feet, she searched for her own keys, her hands trembling as she sifted hurriedly through the clutter on the table—Nick's antique toys, a newspaper, loose change.

Seriously, Nick. Why do you keep all this here?

Finally, her fingers closed around the keys.

She bolted out the door, locking up without thinking, and slid into the driver's seat. As she started the car, she whispered, "Please be okay... please be okay..."

Her grip on the steering wheel tightened as her chest constricted. "Please, God, let my husband be okay. I don't know what I'm walking into, but give me the strength to handle it. Amen."

The prayer left her lips in a shaky breath.

Then the tears came.

What if I lose him?

She shook her head.

No. That's worse-case thinking. God has brought us through too much for this to be the end.

Nick was strong, and so was their love.

She whispered one more prayer—this time not just for herself, but for him. "Lord, please... be with Nick. Let him know You are near."

The closer she got to the hospital, the more fear clawed at her.

She parked, barely aware of her surroundings, and rushed inside.

"Excuse me! I'm looking for my husband, Nicholas Owens. I was told there was an accident," she said breathlessly at the reception desk.

The seconds stretched unbearably before the receptionist responded. "Your name?"

"Miranda Owens."

"I'll let them know you're here. Someone will be right out."

Miranda turned, scanning the waiting room. The harsh fluorescent lights buzzed overhead, casting an almost sterile glow on the too-white walls. The faint scent of antiseptic clung to the air. Almost every seat was taken.

Her gaze landed on a mother with a young boy—his arm in a sling. He kept sneaking glances at her.

"Leon! It's not polite to stare," his mother chided.

Miranda forced a smile and sat down. "He's okay. He's not bothering me." She glanced at the boy's arm. "My! What happened to you?"

"I fell at the park," Leon said. "It really hurts. Mommy thinks it's broken. What happened to you? Are you hurt too?"

She swallowed a lump in her throat. "I'm actually here for my husband. He got hurt, but the doctors are taking care of him."

Leon frowned. "How did he get hurt?"

"I don't know yet."

The boy nudged his mom. "I want to pray for him."

His mother smiled. "That's very kind, Leon." She turned to Miranda. "Would you mind if we pray with you?"

Miranda blinked at them, stunned by the offer. A mix of emotions twisted inside her—hesitation, gratitude, something deep and aching that she couldn't quite name.

Would it help?

For a brief second, doubt flitted through her mind. Then, looking at the boy's earnest expression, she realized—he had no doubt.

Maybe she needed that.

"I would love that," she whispered.

Leon giggled as they struggled to figure out how to hold hands with only one good arm. Eventually, Miranda and his mother held Leon's hand together.

"Dear God," Leon began, "Please help my new friend..." He paused, then looked at Miranda. "What's your name?"

"Miranda Owens."

"Right. Please help my friend Miranda Owen's husband get better. I don't like being in the hospital, and I bet he doesn't either. Also, please make my arm feel better. It's driving me nuts. Amen."

Miranda let out a watery chuckle.

Just then, her name was called.

She turned to Leon. "Thank you. That meant the world to me."

"You're welcome."

She followed the doctor down the hall, heart hammering.

"Nick hit a patch of black ice and crashed into a tree," Dr. Winters explained. "His CT scan shows a mild concussion and severe swelling. To give his body and brain the best chance to heal, we placed him in a medically induced coma. We can't say for certain when—or if—he'll wake up. But with time, anything is possible."

Miranda swallowed the sob rising in her throat. She stepped into the room.

The beeping machines, the tubes, the wires—it wasn't him.

The Nick she knew had a laugh that could fill a room. This Nick... looked lifeless.

Her knees buckled, and she gripped the bedside rail.

"He'll wake up," she whispered. "I know he will."

She closed her eyes.

God, I know You have a reason for everything. Please... help Nick.

6

Miranda whispered prayers into the silence, pleading for something—anything—to change. Nick lay unmoving beneath a tangle of wires and tubes, his body still while the machines kept him stable.

Her fingers curled into a fist. *I know You're here, Lord. I know You're in control. But why does this feel so impossible?*

She wiped at her eyes, taking a steady breath.

Her mother's voice echoed in her mind—words from childhood when things felt uncertain. *"When I am afraid, I trust in You."*

Miranda swallowed, her chest tight. Psalm 56:3.

"I trust you, Lord," she whispered, even as her voice wavered. "Please... bring him back to me."

The steady rhythm of beeping monitors filled the space—a cold reassurance that he was still fighting, still there.

She watched him, her throat dry from unanswered prayers. Nurses had quietly slipped in and out, checking his vitals, offering brief, sympathetic smiles before retreating into the hallway. It had all settled into a weary, clinical stillness.

Until suddenly, the stillness shattered.

Miranda tensed as doctors and nurses came running.

"BP's dropping," one of them said, his voice tight.

"Heart rates erratic," another called.

A nurse reached for the emergency call button, but before she could press it, Miranda clasped Nick's hand.

The moment her skin met his, the air shifted.

It was subtle—so subtle that no one noticed. Except for Miranda.

A whisper of warmth pulsed between them, a flicker of something unseen. The overhead light dimmed for the briefest moment, then steadied. The beeping monitor, which had been screaming a warning seconds ago, faded into something calmer, less urgent. Nick's erratic heart rate slowed, leveling into a more stable rhythm.

Miranda gasped softly, but the sound never fully left her lips. A wave of dizziness crashed over her, and the room tilted, the edges of her vision darkening. Her body sagged forward, her fingers still curled around Nick's hand as everything slipped away.

It lasted only a second. A blink.

Then she was back, her head jerking up slightly as her chest tightened. The world around her continued as if nothing had happened. The doctors hesitated, glancing at the screen.

"That's... better," one of them murmured, brows furrowed in confusion.

"His vitals are stabilizing," another confirmed, flipping through Nick's chart. "I don't understand—his BP was crashing just a second ago."

Her hand still wrapped around Nick's, Miranda stayed silent. Her heart pounded in her ears as she watched the numbers even out, as the doctors exchanged wary but relieved glances.

No one questioned it. No one asked *why* the sudden crisis had passed.

The world moved on, as if nothing had happened.

But Miranda knew better.

She sat back slowly, her fingers slipping away from his hand, and exhaled a breath she hadn't realized she was holding. A lingering tremor ran through her limbs, her body still struggling to recover from whatever had just happened.

Whatever it was, it wasn't enough to heal him completely.

But it had been enough to keep him here.

For now, that was all she could ask for.

7

Miranda was alone with Nick once more, the frantic chaos from earlier now a distant hum echoing in her mind. Hours had passed—how many, she wasn't sure—and exhaustion settled heavily into her bones. Her legs ached from endless waiting, her spine stiffened from the uncomfortable hospital chair. She stretched slowly, the quiet crack of tension releasing did little to ease the deeper restlessness within her.

She couldn't shake the strange feeling that lingered from before—that momentary warmth, the inexplicable shift she'd felt when she'd touched Nick's hand. But the longer she sat in the quiet, sterile room, the more distant the moment felt, slipping away like a half-remembered dream.

Her gaze drifted toward the window, though she wasn't really looking at it. She was too focused on the wave of dizziness that suddenly washed over her. It was quick, barely a moment, but enough to make her steady herself on the chair's armrest. She shook her head, blinking a few times to clear the fog.

"I'm just tired," she murmured to herself, though the words didn't quite settle the unease that was creeping up her spine.

The feeling persisted as she turned back to Nick. His pale face, bruised and battered, stirred something deep within her. She hadn't let herself admit how afraid she was, but now, with the chaos of the last few hours settling, that fear was beginning to take root.

She reached for the water bottle on the small table beside her, her hand trembling slightly as she unscrewed the cap. She took a long sip, the cold water refreshing but doing little to shake the growing sense of nausea that seemed to hang at the back of her throat.

Her fingers brushed the side of her neck absentmindedly, feeling a slight stiffness she couldn't recall having earlier. Maybe she'd been tense this whole time. She had been under a lot of pressure, hadn't she? Between Nick's accident and the hospital chaos, it made sense.

But as she pressed her hand gently to her temple, she felt another wave of dizziness hit her, stronger this time. Her vision blurred for just a moment. She steadied herself, reaching out to grab the edge of Nick's bed for balance. Her heart began to race, and a knot tightened her stomach.

"Okay, this is ridiculous," she whispered to herself. "I can't get sick. Nick needs me. Now is not the time to fall apart."

A faint discomfort in her abdomen made her pause. It wasn't pain, just a strange pressure, a sensation that felt out of place. A thought flickered across her mind—something wasn't quite right.

I'm just stressed. Maybe eating will help.

Her hand briefly brushed over her stomach again before she forced herself to shake off the thought. She walked out into the hallway, trying to focus on something—anything—other than the tightness in her chest and the growing confusion that nagged at her.

Miranda found the nurses' station and approached slowly, hoping for a moment of normalcy, something to anchor her. The nurse behind the desk gave her a warm smile, but Miranda felt a slight, unexplainable tension in the air as she asked, "Do you have anything light to eat? Maybe some fruit?"

Miranda hesitated for a moment, feeling her stomach flutter uncomfortably. It wasn't hunger—it was something else, something harder to name. "I'm not really hungry," she admitted, rubbing the back of her neck. "I think I'm just a little... on edge. I think I've been running on stress for hours and I'm starting to feel like I can't catch my breath."

The nurse gave her an understanding look, her voice gentle. "We hear that a lot. It's easy to forget about yourself when you are focused on someone else." She gave a reassuring smile as she handed Miranda a small napkin and an apple.

Miranda took them, her fingers still trembling slightly, but she appreciated the simplicity of the gesture. She inhaled a slow breath, the familiar scent of the apple a small distraction from the tight knot in her stomach. "Thank you," she said quietly, almost more to herself than the nurse. "I guess... I just need a moment, but I can't seem to find one."

The nurse gave her a soft knowing smile. "Take all the moments you need, even if it's just one small step at a time. You're doing your best, and that's enough."

Miranda nodded, her grip on the apple tightening slightly as she walked back toward Nick's room.

As she passed the intersection near the vending machines, something—someone—moved just beyond the edge of her vision. A shape. A shadow. Watching.

She turned her head, heart thudding once, hard.

Nothing. Just the hum of fluorescent lights and the soft click of distant footsteps.

"You're exhausted," she whispered to herself, forcing another bite of apple past the knot in her throat.

Still... she didn't slow down.

By the time she reached Nick's door, the moment had dissolved. But not completely.

It wasn't much, but the taste of the apple and the rhythm of her steps were just enough to ground her in a moment where everything else felt out of control.

8

Miranda hadn't moved from Nick's side since last night. After the nurse's kindness and a few bites of the apple, she'd forced herself back into the quiet of his room, determined not to succumb to her anxiety. She'd whispered countless prayers into the silence, each one a plea for strength. Eventually, exhaustion overcame fear, and she drifted into a restless sleep with her fingers curled gently around Nick's hand.

A knock at the door stirred her from her daze. She straightened, blinking away the heaviness in her eyes as Dr. Winters and a nurse stepped inside.

"Good Morning Mrs. Owens," Dr. Winters greeted as he did a quick check of the monitors. "We're going to do another CT scan so we can see how his brain is doing."

Miranda sat up a little straighter. "Okay," she said, her voice soft but steady. "Do you think there's been a change?"

Dr. Winters hesitated just a second before answering. "We're hopeful. It's been over twenty-four hours since the last scan and sometimes the swelling starts to go down on its own. We want to see where we're at."

Miranda nodded, running her thumb over the back of Nick's hand. "Is it dangerous to move him?"

"No," he assured her. "We'll keep him stable, and the scan itself won't take long. We just need a clear picture."

Miranda exhaled, glancing at Nick's face. He looked so peaceful, almost as if he were just sleeping. A memory flickered in her mind—Nick laughing, his eyes crinkled with warmth as he held her close during last year's snowfall. He loves winter and everything about it. A small pang of longing tightened in her chest.

"Will we be able to wake him soon?"

Dr. Winters offered a small, careful smile. "If the swelling has gone down, that's a good sign. But we'll still have to take things one step at a time."

She nodded. One step at a time. She rubbed her temple, still unsettled by the faint nausea that had lingered since yesterday.

Just then, two orderlies entered the room. The nurse adjusted Nick's IV, and Dr. Winters placed a reassuring hand on Miranda's shoulder.

"We'll take good care of him," he said gently.

Miranda forced a smile and stood, stepping back as they prepared to move Nick's bed. She brushed a hand over his forehead and leaned down, her voice barely above a whisper. "I'll be right here when you get back," she murmured.

Then she stepped aside, watching as they carefully maneuvered him out of the room.

As the door shut behind them, silence settled around her. The chair suddenly felt too empty.

So she did the only thing she could do.

She prayed.

Lord, You know my heart. You know my fears, my hopes, my every silent plea. I'm placing Nick in Your hands, trusting that You are with him even when I cannot be. I don't know what the results will say, but I know You are greater than any diagnosis, any uncertainty, any storm. Please, Lord, let there be healing. Let there be hope. No matter what comes next, I will praise You. But please... bring him back to me. Amen.

9

A soft knock on the door pulled Miranda from her thoughts. She blinked, the weight of her prayer still heavy in her heart as she rose to her feet.

When she opened the door, she was met with the kind eyes of Leon and his mother, both holding small bouquets of flowers.

"Mrs. Owens? We never officially introduced ourselves. My name is Evelyn Williams," Leon's mom said gently, offering a warm sympathetic smile. "We wanted to check on you."

Leon, shifting the flowers in his hands, added, "And see how Mr. Owens was doing."

Miranda's breath caught slightly at their kindness. She had braced herself for the loneliness of the waiting, but here they were, bringing warmth and support when she needed it most.

"Oh... thank you," she said softly, stepping aside to let them in.

Leon held out his flowers first. "These are for you. Mom said white flowers mean hope."

Evelyn nodded as she handed over her own bouquet. "And these are for Nick. I figured when he comes back, he should have something waiting for him."

Miranda swallowed against the lump in her throat. "This is so thoughtful. You didn't have to—"

"I wanted to," Leon interrupted firmly, his young face set with determination.

A small, grateful smile broke through Miranda's exhaustion. "They just took him for another CT scan, but he shouldn't be gone long. You can stay and visit if you would like."

Evelyn placed a comforting hand on Miranda's arm. "Then that's what we'll do. You won't have to wait alone."

Miranda exhaled, the tension in her shoulders easing just a little. "I'd really like that."

She turned, setting the flowers on the small bedside table before motioning to the chair and loveseat. "Come, sit," she said, her voice steadier now.

Taking a seat back in the chair she'd been in all night, Miranda let out a deep sigh, the weariness of the past few days catching up to her. She glanced over at Leon, holding his blue cast with some discomfort.

"How are you feeling, Leon?" she asked softly. "I see you have a blue cast now."

Leon gave a half smile. "Yeah. Blue's my favorite."

Miranda nodded, watching him for a moment. "You know... you remind me a little of someone."

"Mr. Owens?" Leon guessed.

She hesitated, then smiled gently. "In some ways, yes."

There was a quiet beat before Evelyn softly asked, "Have the doctors said when they'll try to wake him?"

Miranda glanced at the empty space where Nick's hospital bed had been, her heart tugging at the sight. "Soon, I think," she said softly. "They're waiting for the swelling to go down before they bring him out of his sedation."

She paused, pressing a hand to her chest. "But something inside me says he's still in there. Like he's not far... just waiting for the right moment."

Leon's eyes lit up. "Like an angel?"

Miranda's breath caught. She looked at the boy in front of her, so small and yet so full of quiet wisdom. "Yeah," she whispered. "Maybe exactly like that."

Leon hesitated before murmuring. "Mr. Owens... I feel like I know him, even though I don't."

Miranda tilted her head slightly. "What makes you say that?"

Leon fidgeted. "I don't know... It's just a feeling. Like he's some-one I've heard about before. Someone really important."

Miranda's heart skipped. She knew children had a way of seeing things adults could not. She smiled gently. "That's interesting, Leon. I think he'd like you."

Leon opened his mouth as if to say something else, then suddenly shifted. "Did you know I can wiggle my fingers in the cast? The doc-tor said I shouldn't do it too much, but look!" he flexed his fingers, slightly, then winced. "Okay, maybe not that much."

Miranda chuckled. "That might be a good idea."

Leon glanced down, tracing his finger over his cast. "Do you want to sign it?"

Miranda rummaged through her purse for a pen and grinned. "I'd be honored. What do you want me to write?"

Leon thought for a moment. "How about, 'To the best basket-ball player who never got to finish the game.'"

Miranda raised an eyebrow. "A bit dramatic, don't you think?"

Amusement sparked in his eyes. "Hey, it's true."

She shook her head with a smile and wrote: "To the future MVP. You'll be back on the court soon enough! -Miranda" She finished with a small heart and put the pen back in her purse. "There you go. You're officially a legend."

Leon beamed at his cast like it was a trophy.

Evelyn watched quietly, then shifted her gaze to Miranda. "You're really good with him."

Miranda looked up, surprised. "Oh—I just..." She trailed off, un-sure how to explain the flicker of peace she felt around the boy.

Evelyn tilted her head. "You've got that presence. The kind peo-ple lean into when they're hurting."

Miranda swallowed, her throat tight. "Thank you."

Evelyn's voice softened. "I hope someone's doing the same for you."

That time, Miranda didn't answer. Another wave of dizziness washed over her. She pressed a hand to her forehead, trying to steady herself.

Evelyn's brow furrowed. "Miranda... are you okay?"

Miranda quickly nodded. "Yeah, just a little tired. Nothing to worry about."

But the queasiness lingered—harder to ignore now. She forced a smile, not wanting to worry Evelyn or Leon. Still, deep down, she couldn't shake the feeling that something more was going on.

10

It felt like barely any time had passed when Nick was wheeled back into the room.

Miranda rose slowly, still unsteady from the dizziness that lingered from earlier, but the sight of Nick returning pushed everything else aside. The squeak of wheels against polished floors broke through her thoughts as Nick was carefully guided back into place, machines humming softly around him.

Dr. Winters stood at the foot of Nick's bed, reviewing the latest scans on his tablet. "I don't know how to explain this but... the scan we took yesterday showed severe swelling in his brain and we were preparing for the worst. Today it's..." he exhaled, running his hand through his hair. "It's like it was never there."

Miranda's heart pounded, but she forced herself to remain still. She blinked, looking between the doctor and the monitor, letting the weight of his words settle over her. The part of her that had braced for the worst should have been reeling right now—shocked, overwhelmed, questioning how this could be possible. And yet, deep inside, something in her head already knew.

A miracle to everyone else, yes. But to her it was something more.

Leon, who had been quietly standing by glanced at his mom, then turned back to Miranda. "Is everything okay now?" he asked, his voice filled with concern.

"We can't explain it, but yes, we'll keep monitoring him of course. Run more tests. But..." Dr. Winters said as he shook his head in disbelief, his eyes scanning the results again. He had been a doctor for over twenty years. He had seen recoveries he couldn't explain, but nothing like this. Swelling like that didn't just vanish overnight. It didn't just... disappear.

"As of right now, there's no medical reason to keep him in the coma. We can start the process of waking him up."

Miranda's fingers tightened around Nick's hand. She had known this moment was coming, but hearing it aloud still sent a rush of emotion through her. Relief. Gratitude. Awe.

Evelyn placed a gentle hand on Miranda's arm. "That's incredible," she said softly.

A tear slipped down Miranda's cheek, and she quickly wiped it away. "I'm just... I'm just so grateful he's still fighting."

"We'll let you have some time," Evelyn said gently. "We'll check in later. Don't hesitate to call if you need anything."

Leon gave Miranda a hug before they left the room.

Dr. Winters lingered a moment longer. He looked at Nick, then back at Miranda, as if searching for an answer beyond science. "I don't know what's happening here," he admitted. "But in all my years, I've never seen anything quite like this."

Miranda met his gaze steadily, her fingers still curled around Nick's. "Maybe it's not something meant to be explained."

Dr. Winters exhaled sharply, as if he wanted to say more, but instead, he gave her a small nod before stepping out of the room.

The silence settled around her as she turned back to Nick. She watched him closely, her thumb brushing against his skin. He was still so still, but she knew—**not hoped, not wished, but knew**—that he wasn't gone. He was fighting his way back to her.

She closed her eyes, lowering her head.

Lord, I know Your hand has been over us through all of this. I don't understand the how or the why, but I know You were here, guiding, protecting. Thank you for keeping Nick safe, for bringing him back when the doctors had no answers. I trust that whatever comes next, You'll give us the strength to face it. Please, when he wakes, let him remember. Let him know how deeply he is loved. Let him find his way back to himself... and back to us.

She wiped at her eyes, exhaling softly.

"You hear that, honey?" she murmured, her voice thick with emotion. "It's time to come back to me."

Thank you, Lord!

11

Hours had passed since they turned off Nick's sedation, but Miranda felt suspended in time, exhaustion battling hope within her.

Miranda traced slow circles over the back of his hand with her thumb. "I'm right here, sweetheart," she whispered. "Take your time, but I'm waiting for you."

At first, there was nothing. Just the rhythmic rise and fall of his chest. Then, almost imperceptibly, his fingers twitched against her palm.

Miranda gasped, sitting up straighter. "Nick?"

The movement had stilled, and for a moment, she wondered if she had imagined it. But then his fingers curled slightly, weak and slow, like a reflex just beneath the surface of consciousness.

A nurse glanced over and offered a reassuring smile. "That's a good sign. His body is responding."

"Come on, honey, keep going," she encouraged. Squeezing his hand gently.

Everything was heavy. His body. His head. His thoughts.

Nick drifted in and out of something deep and endless, like being underwater, but somewhere far away, warmth wrapped around his hand. It was comforting. Familiar.

He fought to surface, to push past the fog thick in his mind. He didn't know where he was, but something about the way his body ached told him that waking up might hurt.

A voice. Soft. Close.

"Nick?"

The name echoed, but it didn't quite land. Was that his name? He thought so, but there was a hesitation in his mind, like reaching for something just out of grasp.

His fingers twitched—he felt them move, but it wasn't intentional. Something about that warmth around his hand pulled him in, urging him forward.

A new voice. Clinical. Unfamiliar.

Something about a car accident. A coma.

He swallowed, his throat raw and dry. He forced his eyelids open, but the light was too bright, the images too sharp against the blur in his head. Slowly, a shape formed—a woman.

She was close, watching him, her eyes wide with something that looked like hope. She had soft features, long red hair, and there was something in the way she looked at him that made his chest tighten.

He should know her. Shouldn't he?

His mouth was so dry it felt like sandpaper scraping together when he tried to speak. He forced the question out, his voice barely a whisper.

"Who...?"

The way her expression crumbled sent a jolt of unease through him.

"Nick... it's me," she whispered, her voice trembling. "It's Miranda."

The name meant nothing. Only hollow emptiness. Panic flared.

"I... I don't remember."

Miranda forced herself to breathe, even as her heart cracked.

He doesn't know me. He doesn't remember us.

Dr. Winters gave her a reassuring glance before turning back to Nick. "Try not to panic. Memory loss after a traumatic brain injury can be temporary. We'll run more tests and take this one step at a time."

Nick licked his lips, eyes darting around the room as if searching for something, anything, to hold onto. "I don't... I don't remember anything."

Miranda squeezed his hand again, steadying herself. "It's okay. You've been through a lot. I'm here, and we're going to figure this out."

His eyes landed on her, hesitant, searching. "You're my wife?"

Miranda forced a small smile, even as her eyes burned with unshed tears. "Yes."

Nick swallowed hard, looking lost. "I'm sorry," he whispered. "I just... I don't remember."

Blinking back the tears threatening to fall, she held onto his hand a little tighter. "That's okay. You just rest. For now, I'll remember for the both of us."

His eyelids fluttered shut again, his breathing evening out as exhaustion pulled him under. Miranda brushed a shaky hand over her eyes. He was awake, yet he didn't remember her.

"Mrs. Owens," Dr. Winters said gently, stepping closer, "let's talk about next steps."

She nodded, her gaze lingering on Nick's sleeping face.

"As I mentioned, memory loss after a traumatic brain injury isn't uncommon. It could be temporary, but we won't know the full extent until we do further neurological evaluations." His tone was calm, reassuring, but Miranda still felt a pit form in her stomach.

"How long could it take?" she asked quietly, afraid of his answer.

"We'll run more tests, but recovery timelines vary greatly. Patience is key," Dr. Winters said gently.

Miranda nodded, her fingers brushing against Nick's hand. "So, what should I do? Talk to him? Show him pictures?"

"Yes, but don't overwhelm him." Dr. Winters advised. "Small, simple things—stories, familiar scents, music he liked. Sometimes memories return in pieces, like puzzle fragments coming together. Other times, they come back all at once."

Miranda chewed her lip, her heart aching at the uncertainty of it all. "And if they don't?"

The tension around Dr. Winter's eyes faded. "Then we work with where he is now. But let's take it one step at a time."

She let out a slow breath.

One step at a time.

Nick shifted slightly in the bed, his brows twitching as though he were dreaming.

"You've been here for over twenty-four hours," Dr. Winters reminded softly. "You need rest."

"I'm fine."

"Go home—shower, eat. Even a few hours would help."

Miranda hesitated, fingers tightening around Nick's hand. What if he woke up without her there?

As if reading her mind, Dr. Winters continued. "The nurses will be in and out, and I'll check in personally. If there's any change, you'll be the first to know."

She let out a slow breath. "Just for a little while."

Dr. Winters nodded approvingly. "That's all I'm asking."

Miranda looked back at Nick. "I'll be back soon, honey," she whispered. "I promise."

She hesitated a moment longer before finally forcing herself to stand. She felt the weight of exhaustion settle over her immediately. Maybe Dr. Winters was right.

Lord, I place Nick in Your hands. Watch over him while I rest, and give me strength to trust Your plan. Thank you for never leaving us. Amen.

She took a steadying breath, pressing a gentle kiss to his forehead.

"I love you," she whispered, then turned to go, knowing everything happens in God's time.

12

Arriving home, Miranda let the weight of the last twenty-four hours finally release. The silence of the house wrapped around her, so different from the steady beeping of the hospital monitors. She almost turned back, the urge to be beside Nick nearly overpowering her resolve to rest. But exhaustion—and Dr. Winter's firm reminder—won out. She kicked off her shoes, rubbing her tired eyes as exhaustion settled deep in her bones. Her legs felt weak, every step heavier than the last, as the quiet closed around her.

She knew she needed to rest, but her mind still raced—Nick was alive, awake, yet a stranger to her. She whispered to herself, "One step at a time."

With a deep breath, she headed for the shower, hoping the warm water would wash away the tension clinging to her. Just for a little while, she needed to let go.

But as she passed through the living room, the sight of his jacket slung over the arm of the couch stopped her in her tracks. She had told herself she wouldn't break down, that she'd hold it together. But there it was—his jacket, the one he had shrugged off two nights ago like it was any other evening. Now it felt like a relic from another life.

Her eyes burned as she forced herself to keep walking. In the kitchen, Nick's favorite coffee mug sat next to the sink, the faintest ring of dried hot chocolate at the bottom. She swore she could still see the ghost of his fingerprints smudged along the side.

She braced herself against the counter, gripping the edge as a wave of dizziness washed over her. Her body was screaming for rest, but her mind wouldn't stop cataloging everything he'd left behind—his reading glasses on the end table, the book he had been halfway through, still open, still waiting for him.

A soft chirrup broke the silence.

Miranda turned just as Tinsel padded into the room, her movements graceful and unhurried. The tabby cat blinked up at her with those perceptive golden eyes, tail curling around Miranda's ankle like a tether.

"Hey girl," Miranda murmured, sinking down to her knees. Tinsel leaned into her, purring low and steady, as if trying to press reassurance into her skin.

Miranda let her fingers drift through the familiar fur. "It's just us for now," she whispered. "But he's coming back. I have to believe that."

Tinsel gave a soft flick of her ear and nudged Miranda's hand with her head, then hopped lightly onto the counter—her silent way of standing guard.

With shaking hands, she turned away from the kitchen and made her way to the bathroom.

The moment she stepped inside, she let out a shaky breath. She turned the water on and stripped off her clothes, barely noticing the way her fingers trembled as she pulled her sweater over her head.

Steam curled around her as she stepped under the hot spray, the warmth seeping into her skin. The tension in her muscles should have melted away, but it didn't. If anything, the weight in her chest only grew heavier.

She pressed her forehead against the cool tile, letting the water pound against her back. She wanted to cry, to let herself sink into the grief of everything she feels she's losing. But the tears wouldn't come.

Nick was still here. But at the same time, he wasn't.

After what felt like an eternity, she shut off the water and grabbed a towel. Moving on autopilot, she dried off, pulled on a pair of pajamas, and padded toward the bedroom.

The scent of his cologne clung faintly to the sheets as she pulled back the covers—a cruel reminder of what was missing.

She slid beneath the blankets, curling onto her side, willing sleep to take her. But even as exhaustion weighed her down, she found herself reaching for the space where Nick should have been.

And for the first time since the accident, the house no longer felt like home. Sleep finally took her, but there was no peace in it.

She was in the car with Nick. Snow swirled outside the windshield, thick and endless, cocooning them in white. His hands were on the wheel, steady and sure but something felt wrong.

"Nick," she said, her voice swallowed by the storm. "Slow down."

He didn't answer. His eyes stayed fixed ahead, blank, unreadable. The road was disappearing under the snow, the lines vanishing, swallowed by the ice.

"Nick, please—"

The tires skidded. The world lurched sideways.

Miranda's stomach flipped as the car spun out of control. Trees blurred past, dark shadows in the storm. She reached for him, but her fingers passed through his arm like mist.

She screamed his name.

The impact never came. Unsteady, everything went still.

She turned. Nick was gone. The driver's seat was empty.

Panic clawed at her throat. She yanked at the seatbelt, scrambling to escape, but the door wouldn't open. Then, in the rearview mirror, she saw him.

Not Nick.

A stranger in the backseat. Watching her.

His face was shadowed, indistinct, but she knew—deep in her bones—he wasn't supposed to be there.

The air turned ice-cold. The whisper came, low and taunting.

"I know the truth."

A sudden breath caught in her chest.

The figure leaned in closer, his voice twisting around her like smoke.

"It's only a matter of time."

A rush of wind slammed against the car, shaking it violently. Snow pressed in on all sides, suffocating, burying her. The doors groaned under the weight, trapping her inside.

"Soon, everyone else will too."

The words sent ice through her veins.

She gasped, sitting bolt upright in bed.

Her chest heaved as she sucked in ragged breaths, her hands fisting the damp sheets. It took a moment for her mind to catch up to reality. The storm was gone. The stranger was gone.

But she wasn't alone.

At the edge of the bed, Tinsel crouched low, her eyes fixed on Miranda with unnerving focus. Her ears were pinned back, fur bristled slightly—not from fear, but alertness.

She had felt it.

Miranda reached out with a trembling hand. "It was just a dream," she whispered.

But Tinsel didn't move.

A heartbeat passed. Then another. Slowly, the cat slinked forward and pressed her forehead to Miranda's chest, a soft, deliberate touch. Her purr came slow and steady, deeper than before.

Protective. Ancient.

Miranda closed her eyes, drawing a breath as Tinsel's warmth bled into her skin.

Whatever it was... it hadn't been just a dream.

13

Miranda arrived at the hospital the next morning, the dream from the night before still clinging to her like an icy shadow. She shivered slightly as she entered Nick's room, the image of the faceless stranger and his whispered threats lingering, refusing to fade entirely.

She forced herself to shake it off, pushing away the haunting images. Nick needed her present, clear-headed—not lost in nightmares.

When he turned his head and saw her standing by the door, his eyes briefly flickered with recognition.

"Miranda?" Nick's voice is soft, tentative, as if testing the name on his lips. He blinked a couple of times as though trying to place her.

Her heart skipped at the sound of her name. She moved closer, her voice shaking with emotion but steady. "Yeah, it's me. I'm here."

A flicker of warmth passed through Nick's eyes, but the confusion lingered. "I remember... I remember you from last night, but... that's all. I don't remember anything before that."

Miranda's throat went tight. "That's okay. You've been through a lot over the last few days. You don't have to remember everything right now."

Nick looked at her, searching her face for some kind of reassurance. "How did I even get here?"

She sat beside him on the bed, her heart heavy, but she kept her expression steady. She reached for his hand, giving it a light squeeze as she tried to hold back the rush of emotion. "You were in an accident."

Nick's eyes searched hers, confusion still clouding his gaze. "I don't remember any of that. Was anyone else hurt?"

"No," she whispered, a stray tear slipping down her cheek. "You hit a patch of black ice... and hit a tree."

Dr. Winters walked in just then, his expression thoughtful. He glanced at the monitor to check Nick's vitals before turning to Miranda. "How's he doing?"

"He remembers me from last night," Miranda said quietly. "But not much else."

"That's a good sign," Dr. Winters said. "His memory is still fragmented, but at least he recognizes you, which is a step in the right direction."

Nick turned his head towards Dr. Winters. "How long will it take? To get it all back, I mean?"

Dr. Winters shook his head. "It's hard to say, but the fact that you're showing improvement so quickly is promising. Some people remember everything within a few weeks, others take longer."

Nick looked at Miranda, a mix of frustration and fear on his face. "I don't want to forget. I want to remember... everything."

"You will," Miranda said softly. "We'll take it slow, one day at a time. I'm not going anywhere."

Dr. Winters nodded, offering a small smile. "You're doing great. We'll keep you here for a few more days of observation. As long as everything continues to improve, we'll send you home soon."

Miranda sat beside Nick's bed, watching him stare absently at the ceiling. She reached for his hand again, needing the comfort as much as she intended to offer it. But her mind slipped back to the dream—the empty driver's seat, the whispered promise of exposure. It felt disturbingly real, the line between nightmare and reality blurring dangerously. She squeezed Nick's hand gently, grounding herself in the warmth of his skin against hers. One crisis at a time. She couldn't lose herself now—not when he needed her most.

The nurse had come and gone, adjusting Nick's IV and making notes in his chart, but otherwise, it was just the two of them in the room.

Nick lay back in the bed, staring at the ceiling again, his hand resting limply by his side. Miranda watched him, a sadness tugging at her chest. It was one thing to see him physically weak, but seeing him emotionally adrift was a blow she hadn't expected.

"Nick," she said, moving to his side again. "Do you feel okay?"

His eyes flickered towards her, but he still seemed... distant. Like he was trying to piece everything together. "I don't know," he admitted. "I'm just... confused. Like everything is there, but it's too far out to reach."

Miranda's heart ached, and she gently placed a hand on his. "It's okay. You don't have to have it all figured out right now."

He looked at her then, a hint of frustration and vulnerability in his eyes. "I wish I could remember you... more clearly. I wish I knew us. I can feel how much you love me. I just..."

A wave of emotion came over Miranda. She wanted to say *You are my whole world*—the words were right there on her lips. But before she could speak, a sudden wave of nausea hit her. Her stomach turned violently, and she barely had time to stumble into the bathroom, her hand pressed to her mouth to stifle the sensation that surged through her.

"Miranda?" Nick's voice was filled with alarm.

The nausea hit harder this time, leaving Miranda gripping the bathroom sink. Breathing deeply through her nose. *It's just stress. Lack of sleep. Grief.*

Except, she knew better.

She was a midwife. She recognized the signs, had guided hundreds of women through them. But acknowledging it meant accepting that her world was shifting again, just when she needed stability the most.

Not yet. Not now.

She washed her face, smoothing away the exhaustion. Nick needed her. One thing at a time.

She heard the rustle of sheets as she shifted, and a moment later, he was calling out to her, his concern palpable even through the thin walls of the bathroom. "Do you want me to call in a nurse?"

Taking steady, deep breaths to quell the feeling that was returning, Miranda slowly walked back into the room. Her hands were shaking, and she wiped her mouth with the back of her hand, hoping to steady herself. "I'm fine," she managed, each word coming out slow and labored.

Nick's eyes searched her face, his frown deepening. "You don't look fine," he said, his voice laced with worry. "What happened?"

Miranda hesitated, her mind racing with the implications of what she'd just experienced.

"I—I don't know," she finally said, her voice shaky. "I just... I felt sick all of a sudden. It's probably nothing." She tried to convince herself more than him. *I'm just tired and stressed.*

Deep down, something was telling her it wasn't nothing. Something was changing and she couldn't ignore it.

Nick didn't look convinced. "You're sure?" he asked gently, his tone steady but full of concern.

Miranda looked into his eyes, then quickly glanced down, her heart thudding in her chest. She didn't want to say anything—not when he was still recovering, not when he had his own battles to fight. The thought of adding this uncertainty to his already heavy load felt wrong.

"I'm sure," she lied softly, her voice betraying the uncertainty in her eyes. "You are the one we need to worry about. Not me."

She forced a smile, though it didn't reach her eyes. She couldn't let him see how much this moment unsettled her. He needed to focus on getting better—getting back to himself. The last thing he

needed was for her to add this possibility, this burden, to his already
strained heart.

14

Two days later, Miranda folded the last of Nick's belongings into a small duffel bag. The nausea hadn't subsided, and neither had her quiet suspicion she'd carefully hid behind forced smiles and soft assurances. Each wave of sickness was a stark reminder of a reality she wasn't ready to face.

She glanced toward Nick sitting quietly on the edge of the hospital bed, freshly dressed in clothes she'd brought from home. Physically, he looked stronger, healthier even, but the emotional distance in his eyes hadn't diminished. Each time their gazes met, a shadow of confusion lingered—like she was a puzzle he couldn't quite solve.

Dr. Winters had assured her Nick was ready to go home, but the word felt hollow now. Home. Miranda struggled with the concept. It no longer seemed familiar, not when the man who anchored her world was still grasping to recognize who she was, who they were.

She hadn't yet found the courage to tell him her suspicions, determined to protect him from further uncertainty. But as she zipped the duffel bag closed, the weight of keeping secrets pressed heavily against her chest.

She paused, hands resting on the fabric. Her eyes closed, and just under her breath, she whispered, "*Lord, give me the strength to hold this gently. To wait for the right moment. To walk this path even when I feel alone.*"

It wasn't the first time she'd prayed in silence. But this one felt heavier. Like it carried more than just hope—it carried a heartbeat.

"Ready?" she asked, forcing a brightness into her voice that didn't match her feelings.

Nick nodded slowly, eyes uncertain as he stood. "Yeah, I think so."

A gentle knock interrupted the quiet tension. A nurse stepped in with a wheelchair. "Alright Mr. Owens, everything's ready. Just remember to take it easy for the next couple of weeks. No pushing yourself too hard."

Nick let out a humorless laugh. "Hard to push myself when I don't even remember what normal feels like."

Miranda's chest tightened at his words. Silently, she handed him his jackets, noticing the brief hesitation as their fingers brushed. He took it, quickly looking away, a flicker of vulnerability crossing his face.

She watched him ease into the wheelchair, then followed behind, each step toward the exit amplifying the surreal sensation that her life was suspended between two realities—the one she'd known before the accident and the uncertain future that loomed ahead.

Outside, the cold air stung her cheeks as she pointed toward her red Subaru Outback. Her grip tightened around the keys, the nausea flaring again as her mind raced with unspoken fears. She'd tell him eventually—soon. But right now, Nick needed stability, reassurance. Her own uncertainties would have to wait.

15

The sliding doors of the hospital whispered open, letting in a rush of crisp afternoon air as Miranda walked beside the wheelchair, her fingers tightening unconsciously around the handle of Nick's bag. He was quiet—more than usual. The weight of the last few days lingered between them, heavy but unspoken.

She was so focused on him that she didn't notice the man sitting near the window of the waiting area. He didn't move. Didn't fidget. Just sat there, a disposable coffee cup in one hand, his gaze locked on the doors as they disappeared outside.

Wyatt Reynolds took a slow sip, his fingers absently drumming against the side of the cup. He ran a finger over a faded photograph in his other hand. She hasn't aged. Impossible. What kind of trick are you playing Miranda Owens?

He had wondered how long it would take for Nick to be discharged. The reports of the accident had been easy enough to pull—hospital records, not so much. But patience always paid off. He had spent days piecing together the details, watching, waiting, learning. And now, here they were.

His lips curled into the faintest smirk as he folded the newspaper in his lap and set it aside. He didn't need it anymore.

Tossing his barely touched coffee into the trash, Wyatt stood, hands slipping into the pockets of his coat as he strolled toward the exit.

He wasn't in a hurry. He didn't need to be.

They were predictable. And he was good at staying unseen.

16

Miranda hesitated just over the threshold, suddenly aware of how heavy the silence felt. Home was supposed to be their sanctuary, a safe place, but now, it was another reminder of what they'd lost. She stole a glance at Nick, watching closely as his eyes moved uncertainly around the room, looking for something familiar.

Nick hesitated just inside, his eyes sweeping across the space as if seeing it for the first time. In a way, he was. His gaze lingered on the fireplace, the worn-in leather chair that he'd sat in a thousand times before—memories he couldn't grasp.

Before Miranda could respond, a soft thud followed by the gentle jingle of a bell broke the quiet. Tinsel, their gray tabby, leapt onto the arm of the couch, eyeing Nick with her usual unimpressed stare.

Nick blinked. "We have a cat?"

Miranda let out a small laugh, some of the tension in her chest easing. "*I* have a cat. You've spent years pretending you don't like her, but she knows better."

As if to prove Miranda's point, Tinsel hopped onto the back of the couch and stretched, her fluffy tail flicking against Nick's arm. He hesitated, then reached out, running a careful hand over her fur.

"Huh," he murmured, scratching behind her ear as she purred loudly. "I think she likes me."

A mischievous glint lit her eyes. "That's what you always said before claiming she was 'just tolerating' you."

Nick gave a small, almost reluctant smile.

Miranda set his bag down near the door. "Welcome home."

He walked further inside, running his fingers along the back of the couch. "It feels..." He trailed off, searching for the right word.

"Unfamiliar?" she offered.

Exhaling, he rubbed the back of his neck. "Yeah. But not in a bad way. More like...like I should remember."

Miranda's heart clenched, but she kept her voice light. "You will. This place is filled with us. Years of it."

Nick turned to her, studying her as if she, too, was something he was trying to piece together. "Will you show me?"

"Of course."

She reached for his coat, helping him shrug it off. It was something she'd done a hundred times before, something natural, but now, it felt delicate—like handling something fragile. As she hung it by the door, she paused, frowning slightly.

The air in the room felt... warmer. Not the artificial heat from the vents, but something deeper, cozier, like the warmth of a fire even though the fireplace was unlit. She glanced toward it, then back at Nick.

"You feel that?" she asked curiously.

Nick looked at her, brow furrowed. "Feel what?"

"This... warmth. It's like the house knew we were coming home."

Nick opened his mouth to respond, but then he stopped, tilting his head slightly. Now that she mentioned it, he did feel it. The kind of warmth that settled in your bones, comforting, familiar. Like being wrapped in a thick blanket after coming in from the snow.

But that didn't make sense. The house had been empty for days, the heat turned down. And yet...

He shook his head, dismissing the thought. "Maybe you're just happy to be home."

Miranda narrowed her eyes at him but didn't push. Still, the feeling lingered. The unmistakable sense of home, of safety, of something unseen wrapping around them like a shield.

Tinsel leaped onto the back of the couch, stretching luxuriously before curling up. She seemed perfectly content, as if nothing was out of place at all.

Miranda let the moment pass, but deep inside, she couldn't shake the thought—Nick had always made places feel like this. Like warmth, like comfort, like home. Even when he wasn't trying.

She tucked the observation away for later. For now, she was just grateful he was back.

"Do you want to see your woodshop?"

Nick's brows lifted. "I have a woodshop?" A flicker of something—excitement, familiarity—crossed his face before he shook his head. "I mean, I guess that makes sense. It just... feels right."

Miranda smiled, warmth blooming in her chest. "Come on, it's just out back. I'll show you."

They stepped outside, the cool air brushing against their skin as she led him across the short gravel path toward the separate outbuilding tucked behind the house. Behind them, the soft pad of paws followed—Tinsel trotting along at their heels like she knew something important was happening.

The scent of sawdust grew stronger the closer they got. Miranda pulled open the door, motioning him inside. Tinsel slipped past them and immediately leapt onto one of the wooden stools, tail curling neatly around her feet as she observed.

The scent of varnish clung to the air, comforting, and familiar. Nick stepped in slowly, his fingers trailing over the smooth wooden workbench like he was touching a memory just out of reach.

He exhaled slowly. "Wow." His eyes roamed the space, taking in the half-finished projects, the neatly arranged tools, the shelves lined with carefully selected wood. "I did all this?"

She nodded, watching him closely. "You always said working with your hands helped clear your mind."

Nick picked up a small wooden reindeer from the bench, running his thumb over the polished edges. He studied it with quiet reverence, then turned to her with a wry smile. "I think I like whoever I was."

Miranda let out a soft laugh, even as her chest tightened. "You should. He's a pretty great guy."

Before Nick could respond, the sharp buzz of Miranda's phone cut through the moment. She pulled it from her pocket, glancing at the screen. Her heart kicked up.

Charlotte.

She answered immediately. "Hey, Charlotte, what's—"

A low groan and heavy breathing filled the line before a rushed voice interrupted.

"It's happening. Contractions are five minutes apart."

"Daniel! Take a deep breath. Has her water broken yet?"

"No," said Charlotte as she came out of the contraction.

"That means we have a little time but I'm on my way. You've got this momma."

Nick watched as Miranda instantly shifted into a mode he hadn't seen before—calm, steady, completely in control.

"Where are you?" she asked, heading back into the house to grab her coat.

"At home, in the bedroom," Daniel said. "The birth pool is already filled."

Miranda nodded to herself, mentally running through everything she'd need. "Good. Keep the lights low, make sure she's drinking water, and help her breathe. Daniel, remember to relax."

Charlotte let out another low moan in the background.

Warmth wrapped around her words like a quiet reassurance. "You're doing amazing, Charlotte. I'll be there before you know it."

She ended the call and turned to find Nick watching her, equal parts impressed and concerned.

"You do home births," he said, more of a realization than a question.

Miranda gave a quick nod as she threw her birth bag over her shoulder. "Yeah, I do."

Nick ran his hand through his hair, exhaling. "So, that means you're going into someone's actual house to... deliver a baby?"

She glanced at him with a light smile. "Basically. Some families feel safest at home. I run the clinic too, but I'm still on call for home births when they want it."

He shook his head, a small, bemused smile tugging at his lips. "That's incredible."

Miranda paused at the door, something in his voice making her hesitate. "Will you be okay if I go?"

His amusement was quiet, but it flickered bright in his eyes. "Miranda, you're about to bring a baby into the world. I think that takes priority over babysitting me."

Relief washed over her, though she tried not to let it show. "I'll be back as soon as I can."

Just as Miranda turned the doorknob, he called after her, his voice softer this time. "Be careful."

Something in the way he said it, the warmth in his eyes, made her chest tighten. She gave him one last look before she left.

Nick stood in silence, the quiet settling around him, suddenly acutely aware of how alone he truly was.

17

As Miranda drove away, Nick stood by the door for a moment, watching her taillights fade into the darkness. The silence in the cottage suddenly pressed down on him, heavy and unfamiliar. It felt as if the echoes of a life he couldn't remember were whispering just out of reach.

Behind him, a soft thump sounded near the couch. Nick turned to see Tinsel, her ears perked, golden eyes locked on something past the window. Her tail twitched, body stiff with silent alertness.

Nick frowned. "What is it, troublemaker?"

Tinsel didn't blink. Didn't move. She sat eerily still, her gaze fixated on something outside.

Nick exhaled, shaking his head. "Probably a raccoon," he muttered, rubbing a hand over his face. He didn't need to let a jumpy cat feed into his already restless mind.

Grabbing his coat from the hook, he stepped outside. The air was cold, sharp enough to sting his lungs as he breathed it in. He crossed the snowy yard, boots crunching softly, until he reached the woodshop. The door creaked faintly as he pushed it open.

The familiar scent of sawdust and cedar wrapped around him. Inside, the space was quiet and undisturbed—his tools laid out just the way he didn't remember leaving them. Everything felt familiar… but distant, like a story someone else had lived.

He moved to the workbench, running his fingers over the smooth surface. A half-finished project sat waiting—a carved wooden sleigh, still rough around the edges.

Nick picked up a chisel, the handle fitting perfectly in his hand. He ran his thumb over the worn grip, hoping for something to spark—some memory, some connection. Nothing came.

Frustration twisted inside him. Why couldn't he remember something that clearly mattered so deeply? He set the chisel down harder than intended, the sound echoing sharply in the quiet space.

A sharp, sudden hiss cut through the air.

Nick spun around, air catching sharp in his throat.

Tinsel was now standing rigid in the doorway, her back arched, fur puffed out in an aggressive stance. Her ears were pinned flat, and her golden eyes had darkened, locked on something outside.

Nick's stomach twisted. "Tinsel?" he said, cautiously, stepping toward her. "What are you doing out here?"

The cat didn't acknowledge him. She let out a low, warning growl.

A prickle of unease crawled up Nick's spine.

He hesitated, then walked toward the window. The moonlit garden stretched before him, untouched snow glistening beneath the soft glow of the porch light. Nothing seemed out of place.

And yet—

The trees. The space beyond the garden. Something wasn't right.

Nick narrowed his eyes, scanning the edge of the trees through the small window. He wasn't sure what he was looking for—until he saw it.

A figure.

Standing just beyond the garden, cloaked in shadow.

Nick's pulse quickened. His gaze locked on a lone figure at the edge of the garden, half-hidden in darkness.

Nick stepped back from the window, heart pounding. He moved to the shop door, hesitated, then slowly pulled it open.

Cold air rushed in.

He stepped outside.

"Tinsel," he whispered, glancing at the cat still frozen in the doorway. Her ears were flat. Her eyes had not moved from the trees.

Nick took one cautious step onto the path, the snow crunching beneath his boots. "Who's there?" he called, voice sharp in the stillness.

The figure didn't move.

Nick took a hesitant step forward, squinting into the fading light.

Behind him, Tinsel let out a sharp, guttural hiss.

Nick swallowed hard.

"Hello?" he said again, louder this time, urgency creeping into his voice.

Still, the figure remained eerily still, just barely distinguishable from the shadows.

A cold sensation crawled through Nick's chest—not quite fear, not quite recognition, but something eerily close to both.

Then—

The figure raised a hand. A slow, deliberate movement.

Nick inhaled sharply, his breath clouding in the cold. A greeting? A warning?

His heartbeat thundered in his ears as he took another cautious step forward.

And then—without a word, without a sound—the figure turned smoothly, melting back into the darkness of the surrounding woods.

Nick stood frozen, heart hammering, his mind racing.

Behind him, Tinsel let out a long, unrelenting growl before darting away, disappearing back into the house.

The lingering silence pressed down on him, thick with unanswered questions.

He should've gone after whoever it was. Should've done something. But something about that figure—the way they had just stood there, waiting, watching—left a cold, lingering weight in his chest.

Finally, Nick stepped back into the woodshop and shut the door behind him, locking it with a soft click. The familiar scent of sawdust no longer comforted him—it felt thin, hollow, like it couldn't keep the dark out.

He let out a slow breath and pressed his hands to the edge of the workbench.

Alone again, the shop now seemed less like a place of purpose and more like a fragile shelter from whatever waited in the shadows outside.

Tinsel had taken cover beneath the old shelving unit near the far wall, her eyes barely visible, glowing faintly in the dim light.

18

Miranda stood in the dimly lit bedroom, the soft sound of breathing and the occasional wince from Charlotte laboring, filling the air. She had been through this a thousand times, yet each birth still carried a weight, a sort of sacredness, that she couldn't shake.

As she dried her hands and moved to Charlotte's side, Miranda closed her eyes for a breath.

Be with us, she prayed silently. *Steady my hands. Steady her heart. Let this child arrive safely.*

It wasn't a ritual. It was just part of who she was—woven into the rhythm of her work.

Charlotte gripped Miranda's hand, squeezing it through the next contraction. "You're doing great, just breathe," Miranda encouraged.

The other side of the bed, Daniel stood nervously, watching his wife with a mix of awe and helplessness. He had been pacing but now his hand rested on his wife's shoulder, offering silent support.

Miranda's phone vibrated in her pocket, breaking the quiet rhythm of the room. She glanced at it briefly, noting the caller ID. *Nick.* Her heart skipped, but she quickly dismissed the thought. There was no room for distractions now.

She gave Charlotte a reassuring smile. "Almost there," she said, her tone gentle but firm.

The phone buzzed again, its vibrations relentless. Miranda's stomach tightened briefly, a flicker of worry darting through her mind. Nick rarely called more than once, especially knowing she was attending a birth. Her hand drifted toward her pocket, hesitation pulsing through her fingers before she stopped herself. *He's fine,* she told herself firmly, pushing down the unease threatening to bloom. *It can wait.*

This was what she did; this was her role. She needed to be fully present, body and mind, for the woman in front of her. She quickly made the decision, turning her attention back to Charlotte, offering soothing words and steady hands to help her through each contraction.

"Breathe, Charlotte. You're doing amazing. Just focus on me."

Miranda reached for her phone, still vibrating insistently in her pocket, and quickly silenced it, slipping it into her bag. There would be time later to see what was going on, time to reassure Nick or explain. But right now, The only thing that mattered was the new life coming into the world, and the woman who needed her here, now, guiding her through the final steps of labor.

The room was quiet except for Charlotte's breathing, the occasional sound of the husband's voice offering support, and Miranda's soft encouragement. The rest of the world felt far away, as if it had disappeared entirely.

The moment was one of the most important parts of her work. A life was about to begin. Nick would have to wait a little longer.

As the minutes ticked by, the room felt charged with anticipation. Miranda could feel the intensity of Charlotte's contractions building, each one more forceful than the last.

"Just one more push, Charlotte," Miranda encouraged softly, her hands gently placed on Charlotte's knees. "You're so close."

Charlotte took a deep breath, sweat beading on her forehead, her body preparing for the final push. For a heartbeat, there was nothing but stillness, and then, with a soft, sudden cry, the baby entered the world.

Miranda quickly scooped the tiny newborn into her arms, her heart swelling with the quiet, profound joy that always came with this moment. "You did it," she whispered, placing the newborn gently onto Charlotte's chest. Charlotte's arms, trembling with exhaustion, wrapped around her child as tears of joy filled her eyes.

It should have been a perfect moment.

The room was filled with the gentle hush that always followed a birth—the kind of stillness that clung to the air like reverence. Charlotte cradled her newborn, tears streaming down her face as Daniel kissed her temple over and over.

Miranda stayed close but quiet, monitoring from the background as the new family bonded.

Then her phone buzzed again. The sound sliced through the calm like a blade.

Miranda's hand hovered over her bag, her fingers curling before she finally reached for it.

A message from Nick lit up the screen.

Nick: Just saw something strange. Not sure what to make of it. Some figure standing outside, just by the edge of the garden. Something felt off. Are you okay?

Her heart dropped.

A figure? In the garden?

She stared at the message, heart beginning to thud, the weight of the words sinking in slowly. That part of the yard wasn't visible from the street—it would take effort to be back there. Intent.

But was this real?

Nick was still adjusting. Still trying to find his footing in a life that didn't feel familiar.

Was he confused? Misreading something?

Miranda wanted to believe it was nothing. Just a shadow. A tree limb. A moment of disorientation. But a part of her gut stirred anyway.

She tapped out a reply

Miranda: Everything's fine. Just finishing up with the birth. I'll check in when I can.

The moment she hit send, she regretted how casual it sounded.

Because she wasn't fine. Not really.

Not if someone had been near their house.

She slipped the phone back into her bag and turned back toward Charlotte, offering a soft smile. But the tightness in her chest lingered.

As she knelt to pack her things, her mind was already racing through possibilities, questions stacking on top of each other faster than she could answer them.

Who had Nick seen?

Was it real?

And if it was... what did they want?

19

With Charlotte's birth complete and the night well past midnight, Miranda finally pulled into her driveway, headlights washing over the front yard, casting shadows over the wooden fence and frost-covered path to the porch.

She shut off the engine but didn't move right away.

Someone had been outside. Watching.

Nothing seemed out of place, but a weight pressed against her chest, something instinctually warning her to look closer.

She exhaled slowly.

It's probably nothing. Nick's mind is playing tricks on him.

She wanted to believe that. Needed to.

But... something was drawing her to the garden. Instead of going inside, she stepped out of the car and crossed the yard. Her boots crunching through the snow.

Where would Nick have seen someone?

As she moved towards the garden, the air felt heavier—dense with something unspoken.

Her eyes swept the area that Nick could have been talking about. At first, all she saw was the untouched blanket of snow.

Then—

Footprints.

And next to them-

A half-buried picture. Strategically placed right where the footprints stop.

What?

A shiver—not from the cold—rolled down her spine.

Miranda bent down, hesitating before picking it up. The paper was stiff, weathered with age. As she turned it over, her stomach dropped.

It was her.

Standing beside a man.

Her breath escaped in a slow, unsteady exhale.

I know that man.

Arthur Reynolds.

Her knees nearly gave out. Not because of fear, but because seeing his face again—after all these years—was like ripping open a wound that had never truly healed.

How long had it been since she'd allowed herself to even think his name? Since she'd walked away from that life, choosing Nick without looking back?

Her fingers tightened reflexively around the photograph.

She flipped it over carefully, searching for a date, a clue—something. Nothing.

A familiar queasiness stirred in her stomach, though this time, she knew it wasn't just from unease, but with everything going on she chalked it all down to stress.

But now was not the time to think about that.

There has to be a logical explanation. But... Why leave the photo here? Why not just hand it to her?

Maybe it's from a public archive. Maybe Arthur kept it and someone found it...somehow. But even as she thought it, the unease lodged deeper.

Folding the picture carefully, she tucked it into her pocket. She couldn't tell Nick—not yet.

He was already struggling. The last thing she wants to do is add more stress and confusion to his life.

Forcing herself to push it aside, she made her way back toward the house, her boots leaving their own path in the snow as she climbed the steps to the porch. She took one last glance toward the garden before unlocking the front door and stepping inside.

The warmth of the house wrapped around her, carrying the scent of sanded wood and something faintly spiced—Nick had probably made tea. She locked the door behind her and set her bag down, forcing her shoulders to relax.

"You okay?"

Nick's voice caught her off guard.

She turned, finding him leaning on the doorframe of the kitchen. His hair was tousled, his expression groggy, but his eyes were sharp, watching her.

"I checked the garden since you mentioned someone was outside," she said, keeping her tone even as she shrugged off her coat.

Nick's gaze flickered toward the window. He then pushed off the doorframe and took a step closer. "And?"

"There was someone out there. I'm just not sure why," she admitted.

Nick's brows pulled together. "So I wasn't seeing things."

"No," she said quietly. "You weren't."

A flicker of unease crossed his face. He shifted, rubbing the back of his neck-a tell. He was trying to piece things together.

"You think it was just some kid?" he asked. His voice lacked conviction.

Miranda knew he was hoping for an easy answer. She wanted one too.

"Maybe," she offered. "Or someone just passing through."

"Then why stand there?" Nick frowned, glancing back at the window. "Why not come to the door?"

"I'm not sure," she admitted.

A long beat of silence passed between them. Then Nick pressed further. "Did you see anything else?"

Yeah! Me and Arthur Reynolds. The man I was supposed to marry.

"Nothing worth worrying about."

Nick exhaled, his jaw tightening. "I don't like this," he muttered, stepping to the window. He pulled the curtain back slightly, peering outside. "What if they come back?"

Miranda hesitated, then set a gentle hand on his arm.

"Then we'll deal with it," she said, steady, measured.

Nick looked at her then, his gaze searching. His fingers twitched slightly, like he wanted to take her hand but stopped himself.

She wanted to reach for him too—to bridge the quiet distance that had crept in between them—but her hands stayed at her sides.

He nodded, but the tension in his shoulders didn't ease. "I'm going to check the doors," he murmured, stepping away.

Miranda watched as he disappeared down the hall.

Slowly, she pulled the picture out of her pocket and stared at it again, committing every detail to memory.

Arthur Reynolds.

The man she had left behind.

The man she had once promised forever to.

Why didn't she remember taking this picture with him?

And why had someone left it for her to find?

She pressed the folded photo against her chest, letting out a slow breath.

A ripple of dread stirred in her gut. A reminder. A quiet, persistent nudge.

There were two secrets she had to keep now.

And one of them had just followed her home.

20

The days after the photo was discovered had settled into a quiet rhythm.

Nick's recovery was slow, but there were moments-small flashes of recognition-that gave Miranda hope. He remembered how he liked his coffee. He remembered the way the floor creaked near the fireplace. He even reached for her hand once-only to hesitate, his brow furrowing in frustration.

Still, it was progress.

But even as she focused on helping Nick, her own body had been trying to tell her something. She had ignored the signs for as long as she could, chalking her nausea up to stress, but there was only so much denial could mask.

And now, the time she had been avoiding had finally come.

Miranda sat on the edge of the bathtub, her gaze fixed through the crack in the door, watching Nick. He was still asleep, his breathing slow and even, finally resting after another restless night.

Her fingers trembled slightly as she looked down at the test in her hands.

I don't want to add more to his plate.

Positive.

Clear as day.

A sharp breath escaped her lips. Something deep inside clenched—not just with nerves, but the weight of everything bearing down.

She should be happy. They had always talked about having kids. This was something they had wanted. Dreamed about.

But how could she expect Nick to be excited about a future he didn't even remember building with her?

Her reflection in the mirror caught her eye—wide, uncertain, a woman standing on the edge of something enormous.

How am I going to handle this?

She curled her fingers around the test, closing her eyes briefly. She wanted to tell him. She needed to.

But first, she needed to be sure.

Later that morning when Nick went out on his morning walk, Miranda grabbed her coat and hurried to her clinic. She let herself in through the side entrance, avoiding the main reception. The last thing she needed was questions.

The office was quiet. Lydia wasn't in yet, and for that, she was grateful. She moved quickly setting up the test with practiced hands, but her fingers fumbled slightly as she tried to draw her own blood.

Come on, Miranda. You do this all the time.

A voice broke through her concentration. "Need some help?"

Miranda nearly jumped out of her skin. She turned sharply to find Dr. Anaya Patel leaning against the doorframe, arms crossed, a knowing look in her eyes. "I—I was just—"

Anaya raised a brow. "Doing your own bloodwork?"

Miranda sighed.

Busted.

"I needed to be sure," said Miranda.

Anaya stepped forward, gently taking the equipment from her hands. "Sit. I'll do it."

Miranda hesitated but obeyed, settling on the stool as Anaya expertly found her vein. There was no judgement in her expression—just quiet understanding.

"You know," Anaya murmured as she labeled the vial, "you could have just told me."

Miranda managed a weak smile. "I'm sorry. It's all just... a lot."

Anaya gave her a pointed look. "Well, you're not handling it alone anymore. Now spill. When did the symptoms start?"

Miranda sighed, rubbing at her temple. "A few weeks ago. The nausea started first, but I brushed it off. Then came the fatigue. The dizziness. I kept telling myself it was stress, that I was just overwhelmed with everything happening with Nick... but deep down, I knew."

Anaya nodded, her expression unreadable as she tapped a few notes into the tablet beside her. "And does he know?"

Miranda hesitated, biting her lip. "Not yet. I wanted to be sure before I told him. He's been dealing with so much already."

Anaya scoffed. "Miranda, he's your husband. He deserves to know. And trust me, you're not doing him any favors by keeping this to yourself."

Miranda let out a shaky breath. "I know. I just... I don't know how to tell him. What if it's too much? What if—?

"What if he surprises you?" Anaya interrupted gently. "What if he needs this just as much as you do?"

Miranda swallowed hard, looking down at her hands. "I don't know."

Anaya's voice softened into something warmer. "Then let's start with this—you're not alone in this, okay? No matter how it plays out. We'll confirm everything today, and then you figure out how to tell Nick. And when you're ready, I'll be right here. Do you want to wait here for the results or do you want me to call you?"

Miranda glanced at the clock. If she stayed, she'd have to sit in silence, letting her nerves build up. But if she left, she knew she wouldn't be able to focus on anything else.

"I'll wait," she said softly, rubbing her hands together. "I think I'd rather know sooner than later."

Anaya nodded, grabbing the vials. "Good call. I'll run the test now. It won't take long."

As Anaya left the room, Miranda leaned back, staring at the ceiling, her hands resting lightly over her stomach. A quiet prayer passed through her thoughts.

Please, Lord, give me the strength for whatever comes next.

The quiet in the clinic was unnerving. She wasn't used to being the patient. The sterile scent of antiseptic felt different when it wasn't just part of her daily routine but something personally affecting her. The weight of the exam room pressed in on her, making her shift uncomfortably in the chair.

What am I sitting in here for? I have my own office with a better chair. Mental note, get better chairs. Our clients shouldn't have to sit on these.

She left the room she was in and made her way to her office, greeting the slow trickle of employee's that she walked past. The familiar rhythm of the clinic became apparent—soft conversation, the faint beeping of monitors, the scent of lavender and antiseptic. It was easier to breathe when she was in her space, surrounded by the work that made sense to her.

Settling into her chair, she exhaled slowly, running her fingers over the armrest. The waiting was the hardest part. She wanted to pace, to distract herself, but nothing was going to change the outcome. So instead, she pulled out a patient file, forcing her mind into something else, anything else.

Minutes ticked by, stretching longer with each passing second. Just as she was about to check the time again, there was a soft knock on the door. She looked up to find Anaya standing there, a manila folder in her hands.

Miranda's heart pounded. This was it.

Anaya stepped inside, closing the door behind her. "Results are in."

Miranda swallowed, her fingers tightening slightly on the desk. "And?"

Compassion settled into her gaze as she placed the folder on the desk, tapping it lightly. "You're definitely pregnant."

Miranda exhaled slowly, breath catching in her chest before slipping free. She knew. She had already known. But hearing it confirmed made it real in a way she hadn't been prepared for.

She pressed a hand against her stomach, her fingers trembling slightly. "Okay."

Anaya gave her a small smile. "I can't tell if you want to vomit or break out in tears."

A soft, disbelieving laugh escaped her as she shook her head. "Both. Definitely both."

Anaya pulled up a chair and sat across from her. "That tracks. It's a big deal. But hey, at least now you know."

Miranda rubbed her forehead. "Knowing doesn't make it any less terrifying."

Anaya gave her a knowing grin. "Terrifying, sure. But also exciting, right?"

"Yeah... I think so. It's just—everything feels so out of control right now. Nick, the accident, his memory... and now this? How do I even begin to tell him?"

Anaya folded her arms, her expression thoughtful. "You start by taking a deep breath. And then you remind yourself that this is just as much his news as it is yours. It's not a burden, Miranda. It's your family."

Miranda exhaled slowly, nodding. "You make it sound so easy."

"Not easy. Just necessary," Anaya corrected. "And you don't have to do it alone. You've got all of us in your corner. And you've got Nick—even if he's still putting the pieces together."

Miranda smiled weakly. "Thanks, Anaya. I needed to hear that."

Anaya patted her knee. "That's what I'm here for. Now, when are you going to tell him?"

Miranda exhaled slowly, pressing her fingers to her temples. "I'll tell him soon."

Anaya gave her a long, pointed look. "Define 'soon.'"

Miranda hesitated. "When the moment feels right."

Anaya groaned, throwing her hands up. "You and your 'moments.' Miranda, there's never going to be a perfect time. You just have to rip the bandage off."

"I know," Miranda said softly, glancing toward the window. The sky had brightened, the sun pushing through the morning mist. Nick was probably heading home from his walk by now, and the thought sent a fresh wave of nerves through her. "I just need a little time."

Anaya studied her, then sighed, relenting. "Fine. But don't wait too long. He deserves to know, and you deserve to stop carrying this by yourself."

Miranda nodded, the truth of those words settling deep in her chest. "I promise. Soon."

Anaya pushed to her feet with a lopsided grin. "Just remember, if you keep stalling, I will personally show up at your house and tell him myself."

Miranda huffed a laugh, shaking her head. "Noted."

Anaya winked. "Good. Now take a breath and give yourself a minute. You've earned it." She stepped out of the office, gently closing the door behind her. She barely made it two steps before a voice rang out from behind the nurse's station...

"Well, unless ghosts are suddenly charting in your office... I'm guessing that wasn't just you in there."

Anaya paused, then turned toward the nurse's station. Lydia stood with a coffee in hand, one brow arched and that familiar glint of mischief in her eyes.

"You *do* know Miranda's not supposed to be in today, right?"

Anaya didn't flinch. "I'm aware."

Lydia leaned an elbow on the counter, eyes narrowing just enough to show she was curious—but not prying. Not yet. "Everything okay?"

Anaya lifted the folder in her hand. "Just checking on a friend."

Lydia gave a little hum of acknowledgement, but didn't move. "Well, whatever it is... I'm sure it'll work itself out."

She let it hang there, casual but pointed. Then she smiled and added, "You didn't see me. I didn't see you."

Anaya smirked and walked on. As soon as she rounded the corner, Lydia straightened up and immediately bee-lined for Miranda's office.

She didn't bother knocking. She swung the door open mid-sentence, already charging in. "Listen, if you two are secretly plotting a clinic-wide surprise party and I'm not invited, I swear—"

She stopped cold.

Miranda was at her desk, head resting on her folded arms, her whole body curled inward like she was trying to shrink away from the world. She hadn't even flinched at Lydia's entrance.

The sass drained from Lydia's face in an instant.

"Hey..." she said, gently closing the door behind her. "Mira?"

Miranda slowly lifted her head, her eyes rimmed red, her expression raw.

Lydia stepped closer, voice barely above a whisper now. "Tell me you didn't just get awful news."

Miranda swallowed, voice hoarse. "I'm pregnant."

Lydia blinked. Once. Twice. Then her mouth fell open, and she whispered, "Shut. Up."

Miranda let out a weak, breathy laugh—surprised that she could laugh at all. "I wasn't planning on telling anyone today. Anaya caught me trying to do my own blood work."

Lydia's jaw dropped. "You tried to sneak your own labs? Girl, what were you gonna do—run your HCG and then pretend you didn't see the results?"

Miranda gave her a look, somewhere between sheepish and exhausted. "Honestly? That was the plan."

Lydia sat down in a chair and leaned back, eyes wide. "That is the most emotionally repressed, midwife-in-denial thing I have ever heard, and I love you so much for it."

Miranda rubbed her temples. "I didn't know what else to do. Everything with Nick has been so—" She broke off, pressing her lips together. "Complicated."

Lydia's tone softened instantly. "Hey. I get it. You're carrying a lot."

"I just needed to *know* before I told anyone," Miranda said quietly. "Before I even let myself believe it was real."

Lydia nodded, her usual sass toned down to something gentle. "That makes sense." She was quiet for a moment, then added, "Just don't disappear into your own head, okay? That's where all the worse-case scenarios live."

Miranda's eyes welled up again, unbidden. She blinked quickly, trying to hold it back.

Lydia got up, walked around the desk, and hugged her, squeezing lightly. "Stay here. With me. In the moment. Just for now."

21

Nick walked.

He wasn't sure how long he had been out, but the cold had seeped into his fingers despite the gloves he wore. He barely noticed.

The road stretched ahead, a familiar path leading toward the quiet outskirts of town. He had taken this route before-or at least, he assumed he had. Everything felt familiar and foreign all at once.

The frustration of it sat heavy in his chest.

Some days were better than others. Today was not one of those days.

His memories were still jagged, coming in pieces that didn't fit together. He could recall how he liked his coffee, the feel of wood grain under his fingertips when he worked with his hands-but not why it mattered.

And then there was Miranda.

She was patient. Kind. She spoke to him like a man she had known her whole life, but some days, he felt like a stranger in his own marriage.

Who had I been before all of this?

A sharp wind rushed through the trees, and Nick stopped walking, exhaling slowly.

There were flickers of memory when he was around her. The way her voice could steady something in him. The way his body sometimes reacted on instinct-like when he had reached for her hand the other day without even thinking.

But then, the moment would pass, leaving him feeling adrift.

How long would she keep waiting for him to feel like himself again? How long before she got tired of this version of him-the one that didn't quite fit?

His hands curled into fists inside his pockets.

He didn't blame her for trying to help him. He didn't blame her for looking at him with hope, like one day, everything would just snap back into place.

But he wasn't sure it would.

And that scared him more than he wanted to admit.

The front door creaked open, letting in a gust of cold air as Nick stepped inside. He didn't say anything at first, just shrugged off his coat and set it on the hook by the door. The house was quiet—too quiet.

He rubbed his hands together, trying to warm them, before running a hand through his hair. He had been walking longer than he planned, trying to clear his head, but the quiet in the house felt heavier than usual.

Just as he reached for the kettle, the door opened again.

Miranda stepped inside, her arms wrapped around herself, the cold still clinging to her. She looked up, startled to see him there.

"Oh," she murmured, forcing a small smile. "I didn't think you'd be home yet."

Nick frowned slightly, glancing at the clock. "I didn't realize you had work today."

Miranda nodded, unwinding her scarf, but didn't offer an explanation.

Nick's brows pulled together. "I thought you were taking it easy this morning."

She moved toward the kitchen, avoiding his gaze. "I had some things to take care of."

Nick followed her, his mug forgotten on the counter. He wasn't sure why, but something about the way she said it set him on edge. "What kind of things?"

Miranda's grip tightened on the kettle as she poured hot water into a second mug. "Just... some paperwork, a few patient records to go over." She slid the mug toward him, keeping her expression carefully neutral. "I made tea before I left. Should still be warm."

Nick took the mug, but he didn't drink from it. He studied her instead.

Something wasn't right.

She wasn't lying exactly, but she wasn't telling him the whole truth either.

Miranda never stayed at the clinic this long unless she had a birth, and she hadn't mentioned one. And the way she wasn't meeting his eyes? He knew that look. It was the same one she gave when she was holding something back.

"You're sure that's all it was?" he asked carefully.

Miranda finally looked at him then, her eyes flickering with something unreadable. "Nick, it's nothing."

Nick exhaled, rubbing a hand over his jaw. He wanted to push. He wanted to demand an answer, to shake whatever was weighing on her loose. But he knew better.

She'd tell him when she was ready.

Even if he hated waiting.

For a moment, it was quiet. A normal afternoon.

But it wasn't.

Nick lifted his gaze, something flickering behind his eyes. "Have I always been like this?"

Miranda's breath caught. "Like what?"

Nick exhaled, staring into his cup. "Distant. Like I'm here, but I'm not really here."

She opened her mouth to reassure him, but something in his expression stopped her. He didn't want comforting words—he wanted honesty.

She swallowed. "No. You used to be steady. Certain. But even back then, you carried more weight than you let people see."

Nick hummed, thoughtful. "Sounds about right."

Miranda hesitated, her heart pounding.

This was the moment.

She could tell him now. Just say it.

"Nick, I-"

He looked up, waiting.

Her lips parted, but the words didn't come.

Instead, she shook her head slightly and forced a small smile. "I'm glad you're home."

Nick studied her for a long moment, like he sensed something unspoken lingering between them. But then he just nodded, lifting the cup to his lips.

"Me too."

Silence settled between them again.

Miranda turned away.

She would tell him soon, just not tonight.

22

The next morning Nick stood in the woodshop, staring at the unfinished piece of wood in front of him.

His hands rested on the workbench, fingers curled around the edges as frustration burned under his skin.

I used to know how to do this.

That thought had been circling his mind for days. Weeks. Since the moment he woke up in the hospital bed, blinking against the too-bright lights, his brain full of empty spaces.

Woodworking had been second nature to him. He didn't have to think about it before. The weight of the tools in his hands, the feel of the grain beneath his fingertips-it had all come naturally.

Now, he was hesitating.

He picked up a chisel, rolling it between his fingers before setting it back down.

Nothing felt right.

His grip was wrong. His stance was wrong. It was like muscle memory was trying to kick in, but his brain wasn't cooperating.

Nick exhaled sharply and grabbed a nearby block of wood, intending to make something-anything. His hands moved automatically, but halfway through the first cut, the chisel slipped.

The blade skidded off course, gouging too deep.

Nick cursed under his breath and threw the tool down.

The sharp clatter echoed through the shop.

"Nick?"

He didn't turn around. He didn't want her to see him like this.

"Yeah?" He muttered, rubbing a hand over his face.

A pause. Then, "Are you okay?"

Nick let out a bitter laugh, finally turning to face her. "Not really."

Miranda stepped inside, her arms crossed, her eyes full of quiet concern.

"I thought this would come back naturally," he admitted. "Like riding a bike or something. But I can't even hold a damn chisel the right way."

Miranda glanced at the wood, then back at him. "You've been pushing yourself pretty hard."

"Because I need to! "His voice came out sharper than he intended, and Miranda blinked at him in surprise.

Nick sighed, pinching the bridge of his nose. "Sorry. I just-" He exhaled, searching for words. "I don't feel like myself. And I don't even know if you see me as myself anymore."

Miranda stepped closer, hesitating only for a second before placing a hand on his arm.

"I still see you Nick," she said softly. "Even when you don't."

His jaw tightened. He wanted to believe her. He really did. But the longer this dragged on, the more he felt like a stranger in his own life.

Miranda squeezed his arm lightly before stepping back. "Come inside. Take a break. This doesn't have to come back all at once."

Nick nodded, but doubt still gnawed at him.

Because what if it never came back?

A knock at the door pulled Miranda from her thoughts. She wiped her hands on a dish towel and made her way through the house, peeking out the window to see Evelyn and Leon standing on the porch, bundled up against the early spring chill.

She smiled as she opened the door. "Evelyn! Leon! What a surprise!"

Leon grinned at her, his arm still wrapped in the cast he'd gotten after his fall. "Mom said we should come check on Mr. Nick!"

Evelyn chuckled. "Leon was very insistent."

Miranda stepped aside. "Come in, come in. Nick's out back, but he'll be thrilled to see you."

As she led them inside, the warmth of the house welcomed them. Leon's eyes widened as he took in the cozy space, his gaze landing on the wooden reindeer on the shelf.

"That's cool," he said, pointing. "Did Mr. Nick make it?"

Miranda nodded. "He did. He's made a lot of things around here."

Just then, Nick appeared in the doorway, brushing sawdust from his hands. His gaze landed on Leon, and for a split second, something stirred in his expression—recognition, maybe? But it was fleeting, lost in the haze of his still-recovering mind. He frowned slightly before covering it with a smile. "Hey, kid."

Leon grinned. "I wanted to check on you! And..." He hesitated, looking up at his mom before blurting out, "Can I see your woodshop?"

A hint of mischief curved his lips as he glanced at Miranda. "Sure, if your mom's okay with it."

Evelyn smiled. "Go on. Just don't let him leave with a power tool."

Leon let out an excited cheer, and Nick gestured for him to follow. But as they stepped away, Nick hesitated again, glancing over his shoulder at Miranda, lowering his voice. "I know him, don't I?"

Miranda's chest tightened. "Yeah. You met him at the hospital."

Nick nodded slowly, as if trying to grasp onto the memory, but after a moment, he shook his head and led Leon outside.

Once they were gone, Miranda turned to Evelyn, exhaling softly as she led her to the kitchen. "Tea?"

"That sounds perfect," Evelyn said, settling into a chair.

As Miranda poured the tea, she hesitated. She glanced at Evelyn, her fingers tightening briefly around the cup.

"Evelyn, can I ask you something?" she asked softly.

Evelyn looked up, instantly attentive. "Of course."

Miranda sat down slowly. "You and Leon's dad... were you ever in a place where everything felt unfamiliar? Like you were trying to hold onto something that was already slipping away?"

Evelyn's eyes softened. "Yeah. More than once."

Miranda looked down, voice barely above a whisper. "How did you handle it?"

"I had to stop waiting for things to go back to the way they were," Evelyn said honestly. "I kept holding on so tight to see what we used to be that I almost missed who we were becoming."

That struck something deep.

Miranda exhaled slowly. "It just feels like I'm losing him, piece by piece."

Evelyn reached across the table, her fingers warm over Miranda's. "You're not. You're still in there for him. I see it—in the way he looks at you, even when he's confused. It's like some part of him... knows."

Miranda blinked quickly, swallowing hard. "I keep hoping he'll remember everything. That it'll just... come back."

"Maybe it will. But maybe what matters more is what he's choosing now, even without the memories."

Before Miranda could answer, laughter echoed from the back of the house.

A moment later, Nick and Leon walked in. The little boy was beaming, holding a small wooden bird in his hands.

"Look what Mr. Nick made!" Leon declared proudly.

Nick smiled faintly, his eyes lingering on the boy as though trying to place a feeling he couldn't name. He sat down beside Miranda quietly, the carved bird still clutched in Leon's small hands.

Evelyn gave Miranda a small smile. "See? Maybe you don't need to remind him who he was. Maybe you just need to let him find it on his own."

Miranda didn't reply. She just watched Nick, her hand resting lightly on the table, close to his.

After visiting a little while longer, Evelyn and Leon said their goodbyes, heading out the door. The house fell quiet in their absence, the air settling into something heavier—something neither Miranda nor Nick seemed eager to break.

The sound of silverware against plates filled the silence between them.

Lunch had been quiet. Not uncomfortable, not tense-just heavy.

Miranda stole a glance at Nick across the table. He was eating slowly, his brow furrowed in thought, his mind clearly elsewhere.

She wished she could reach across the space between them. Tell him something-anything-to make him feel like he wasn't alone in this.

But the truth felt too big to say out loud.

Not yet.

"Did you finish that carving you were working on?" she asked, breaking the silence.

Nick's jaw tensed slightly, and he shook his head. "Didn't turn out the way I wanted.

Miranda's voice gentled. "It'll come back to you."

Nick let out a short humorless laugh. "You keep saying that."

She bit her lip.

Because I need to believe it, Nick.

The conversation lapsed again. She hated this. Hated the distance. The weight between them.

His fork hovered over his plate before he set it down, exhaling sharply. "I feel like I should know him."

Miranda blinked. "Who?"

"Leon." Nick rubbed a hand over his jaw, frustrated. "I've never met him, but... I don't know. There's something familiar about him, like I should recognize him. Like I already do."

A shiver crawled up her spine. Nick's instincts were rarely wrong.

"Maybe it's nothing," he muttered.

But Miranda could tell he didn't believe that.

Her hand drifted to her stomach-a thoughtless, natural motion.

Nick's eyes flickered up, catching the movement.

A flicker of emotion froze her mid-breath.

His gaze lingered for a second too long, like he was about to say something.

Then, to her relief, he just took another bite.

She forced her hand away, reaching for her water instead.

Careful, Miranda.

She swallowed hard, forcing herself to stay composed.

But the realization hit her all at once-this was going to get harder.

She could keep her words in check, but her body was already betraying her.

And sooner or later, Nick was going to notice.

23

Miranda had spent the morning buried in paperwork, trying to catch up on administrative tasks that had piled up over the past week. But no matter how hard she tried to focus, something felt... off.

She sat in her office, tapping her pen against her desk, a frown tugging at her lips. It wasn't pain, not exactly. Just a strange awareness in the pit of her stomach, a deep-seated instinct whispering that something wasn't quite right.

Taking a steady breath, she pressed a hand over her abdomen. She wasn't even showing yet, but the life growing inside of her was undeniable. And now, that same life seemed to tug at her thoughts, making her uneasy in a way she couldn't explain.

Maybe she was just anxious. Maybe the weight of everything—the pregnancy, Nick, the uncertainty of it all—was finally catching up to her. But still...

She needed to be sure.

Without overthinking it, Miranda stood and slipped into the hallway. She moved with purpose, weaving past nurses and patients, keeping her expression neutral. No one knew yet. No one could know yet.

She reached Anaya's office and knocked softly before pushing the door open.

Anaya glanced up from her tablet, raising a brow. "What's wrong?"

Miranda stepped inside, shutting the door behind her. "I need a favor."

Anaya immediately straightened, setting the tablet aside. "Are you in pain?"

"No," Miranda admitted. "It's not that. I just... I have this feeling. And I need to check. Just to make sure everything's okay."

Anaya's brows knit together. "A feeling?"

Miranda nodded.

Anaya folded her arms. "Miranda, you're a midwife. You know the clinical signs we look for before ordering early ultrasounds—spotting, cramping, severe nausea, or a history of complications. You haven't mentioned, nor had any of that."

"I know," Miranda said, rubbing the back of her neck. "But this is different. It's not something I can explain."

Anaya's gaze sharpened. "You want me to run a test based on instinct?"

Miranda exhaled slowly. "Yes."

Anaya stared at her for a long moment, her scientist's mind clearly turning over the request. Then, with a sigh, she stood. "You're lucky I like you."

Relief flooded Miranda as Anaya gestured her to follow.

As they walked down the hall, Anaya glanced at her sideways. "For the record, if this turns out to be nothing, I reserve the right to say 'I told you so.'"

Miranda laughed softly. "Fair enough."

She wasn't sure what she was hoping to find, but she knew one thing for certain—she needed to see her baby.

The ultrasound room was dimly lit, the soft glow from the monitor casting a pale blue hue over the walls. Miranda settled onto the exam table, rolling up her shirt just enough to expose her lower abdomen. Despite the warmth of the room, a slight shiver ran down her spine.

Anaya snapped on a pair of gloves, grabbing the bottle of gel. "You do realize you're being a little paranoid, right? There's no indication of complications and you don't have a history of miscarriages. Just your 'feeling.'"

Miranda gave her a pointed look. "Are you going to do this, or are you just going to lecture me?"

Anaya gave her a teasing look but didn't push further. "Fine." She squeezed a generous amount of gel onto Miranda's stomach, the cool sensation making her flinch slightly. Then, with practiced ease, she moved the ultrasound probe into place.

For a few seconds, there was only silence.

Miranda held her breath, her eyes locked onto the screen.

Anaya, ever the professional, kept her expression unreadable as she adjusted the probe, angling it slightly before finally stopping. A soft flickering motion appeared on the screen, a steady rhythm pulsing in perfect time.

A heartbeat.

Miranda exhaled sharply, her fingers tightening around the exam table.

"There's your baby," Anaya murmured, her voice softer now.

Miranda stared at the tiny, barely formed figure on the screen, so small yet so impossibly real. The heartbeat was strong, steady.

She hadn't realized how much she needed this.

A choked laugh bubbled from her throat. "I wasn't imagining it."

Anaya didn't respond right away. Her eyes remained locked on the screen, her fingers adjusting the probe slightly as if she were double-checking something.

Miranda's joy flickered with uncertainty. "Anaya?"

Anaya's lips pressed into a thin line. "The baby's heartbeat is strong."

She released the tension in her chest with a small, relieved laugh. "That's good, right?"

Anaya didn't answer immediately. She tapped the screen, zooming in slightly. "It's stronger than I expected."

Something in her tone made Miranda's stomach tighten. "What do you mean?"

Anaya frowned slightly, her fingers tapping a few numbers into the machine. "At this stage of pregnancy, we expect a heart rate between 110 and 160 beats per minute." She angled the screen slightly, pointing at a set of numbers in the corner. "Your baby is clocking in at 190."

Miranda's mouth went dry. "That's... high."

Anaya nodded slowly. "It's not dangerous per se—some babies naturally have a higher baseline. But it's not typical. Especially not for how early you are."

Miranda swallowed, trying to focus on the sound of the heartbeat. It wasn't frantic, wasn't irregular—it was just strong. Too strong.

"Could it be a machine error?" she asked, grasping for something logical.

Anaya was already ahead of her, resetting the probe and checking again. The steady, rhythmic thump remained unchanged. "Nope. Same reading."

Miranda's hand drifted to her stomach. The unease that had driven her here in the first place stirred again, stronger this time.

Anaya finally exhaled and leaned back slightly. "Look, I don't want to alarm you. If the heart rate was way out of range or irregular, I'd be more concerned. But this? It's just... unusual."

Miranda nodded, though her mind was already spinning. Unusual.

She thought back to how she'd felt lately. The strange pull in her gut, the way her exhaustion was always followed by bursts of energy she couldn't explain.

And now this.

Anaya's gaze flickered toward her. "We'll keep an eye on it. I don't want to stress you out, but I also don't want to ignore it."

Miranda forced a breath through her nose, nodding. "Okay."

Anaya's features gentled. "It's still your baby, Miranda. Healthy, growing. Just... a little different."

Miranda swallowed hard, glancing back at the screen. The tiny, flickering heartbeat pulsed strong, steady.

Anaya shut off the ultrasound machine, wiped down the probe, and discarded the gloves. "Come on, let's talk in your office. I think you need to sit somewhere that isn't covered in medical-grade paper."

Miranda huffed a weak laugh but didn't argue. She followed Anaya out of the ultrasound room, keeping her expression neutral as they wove through the clinic.

Once inside her office, Miranda shut the door and slumped into the chair. She rubbed her temples, trying to ease the tension building there.

Anaya perched on the edge of Miranda's desk, arms crossed. "So."

Miranda glanced up warily. "So?"

Anaya raised a brow. "How did telling Nick go?"

Miranda opened her mouth. Closed it. Looked away.

Silence stretched between them.

Anaya groaned, tilting her head back. "Miranda. Seriously?"

"I was going to," Miranda said quickly, holding up a hand. "I am going to."

Anaya let out a slow breath, pinching the bridge of her nose. "I gave you days."

"I know," Miranda mumbled, avoiding her gaze.

"I threatened you."

Miranda sighed. "I remember."

"And yet, here we are," Anaya said, exasperated. "You still haven't told him?"

Miranda ran a hand through her hair, frustration clear in her face. "Anaya, it's not that simple. Nick is still—he's still putting his life back together. I don't know how he's going to handle this—"

Anaya interrupted, leveling her with a firm look. "You don't get to decide that for him, Miranda. He deserves to know. He needs to know."

Miranda slumped back in her chair, pressing her palms over her face, "I just—"

Her voice broke. She hadn't planned on crying. She hadn't felt like she was going to cry. But the weight of everything hit all at once.

A sob clawed its way up her throat before she could stop it.

"Oh, come on," she whispered, swiping at her cheeks as the tears spilled over. "Not now."

Anaya's teasing expression immediately dropped. "Miranda."

Miranda tried to shake her head, to wave it off, but the more she fought it, the harder the tears fell.

"I don't—" Her voice cracked mid-sentence. "I never cry at work."

Anaya sighed and grabbed the tissue box from the desk, placing it in front of her. "First time for everything."

Miranda sniffed, snatching a tissue and dabbing her eyes. "This is so stupid."

"It's not stupid." Anaya's voice was calm, but there was no arguing with that firm, logical tone. "You're pregnant. Your body is basically a science experiment right now. You're allowed to have a meltdown."

Miranda let out a shaky breath, burying her face in the tissue. "I just feel so out of control."

Anaya nodded. "That tracks."

Miranda groaned. "Why do you sound so unsurprised by this?"

Amusement tugged at Anaya's lips. "Because I saw this coming five days ago when you didn't tell Nick like you were supposed to."

Miranda glared at her over the tissue. "You're enjoying this, aren't you?"

"A little," Anaya admitted. Then, more gently, "But mostly? I just want you to stop torturing yourself."

Miranda swallowed hard, looking down at the ultrasound photo still clutched in her fingers. The tiny heartbeat. The proof of this impossible, unexpected, terrifying miracle.

Her bottom lip trembled, and fresh tears welled in her eyes.

"I don't know how to do this, Anaya," she admitted in a whisper. "I don't know how to be this person."

Anaya softened, reaching out and squeezing Miranda's hand. "You don't have to know. You just have to do the next right thing. And right now? That means telling Nick."

Miranda nodded, still sniffling, still feeling utterly overwhelmed. "I will," she said, voice barely above a whisper.

Anaya raised an eyebrow.

Miranda groaned, wiping her eyes again. "Soon."

Anaya sighed, standing up. "I'm holding you to that. And in the meantime, drink some water. You look dehydrated."

Miranda let out a watery laugh as Anaya left, but the moment the door clicked shut, she pressed the ultrasound picture to her chest and let out another deep breath.

She was having a baby. And no matter how scared she was... she knew one thing for certain. She couldn't keep it from Nick much longer.

24

The morning light streamed through the kitchen window as Miranda poured herself a cup of tea. She was moving slower than usual, exhaustion weighing down her limbs more and more each day. Thankfully Nick didn't seem to notice. Or if he did, he didn't say anything.

He sat across from her, staring into his coffee like he was trying to solve a puzzle.

Miranda had learned to recognize this look. It meant something was stirring in his mind.

She hesitated before speaking. "You okay?"

Nick blinked, as if he had forgotten she was there. Then he looked up, his expression unreadable.

"I... I remembered something."

Miranda's breath caught. "You did?"

Nick nodded slowly, his fingers tightening around his mug. "It wasn't much, but it felt... clear."

She leaned in, heart pounding. "What was it?"

Nick exhaled sharply. "I was outside, chopping wood. It was cold-snow on the ground. I remember you standing on the porch, wrapped in that big red scarf you love."

Miranda's stomach twisted. She knew exactly what day he was talking about.

It had been their first winter in this house. Nick had insisted on chopping wood himself, despite the fact that she had suggested buying it pre-cut. He had grumbled about the knots in the logs the entire time.

And then-

"I remember you laughing," Nick continued, his brow furrowing. "I was frustrated about something—couldn't split a damn log properly. And you... you just laughed at me."

A soft gasp escaped her lips.

He was right.

It had been a rare moment of lightness, one of those simple, warm memories that had meant nothing at the time but felt like everything now.

Nick looked up at her then, his blue eyes searching. "That was real, wasn't it?"

Miranda swallowed past the lump in her throat and nodded. "Yeah, Nick. That was real."

He let out a slow, shaky breath and leaned back in his chair. "It felt different. Stronger. Like it actually belonged to me."

Miranda smiled, but her chest ached.

Because this was what she had been waiting for. For him to start feeling like himself again.

But now, the closer he got to remembering their life together, the harder it became to tell him what she had been keeping from him.

Her hand drifted to her stomach beneath the table, where their future was growing-and he still didn't know.

"Nick," she started, voice barely above a whisper.

He looked up, expectant.

For a brief moment, she almost said it.

But then he spoke first. "Maybe I'm finally getting somewhere."

The hope in his voice shattered her resolve.

She still couldn't tell him. "I think you are."

Hours go by and Miranda gradually starts feeling off. She decides in that moment to take a nap. Hoping that the feeling would pass.

It didn't.

Nick had been making more coffee in the kitchen as she lay on the couch in the living room.

The smell of coffee-normally something she loved- hit her hard, turning her stomach. She pressed a hand over her mouth, breathing through the wave of sickness.

Nick's voice cut through the haze.

"Hey-are you okay?"

Miranda's heart skipped. She forced herself to stand up from the couch, pasting on a neutral expression before turning toward him. "Yeah. Just tired."

Nick frowned, his gaze flickering over her face. He didn't look convinced.

"You're pale," he said, setting down his mug. "And you've barely eaten today."

Miranda waved a hand dismissively. "I'm fine, Nick. It's probably just something I ate."

Nick didn't look away this time.

"You've been off for days." His tone was careful, but his eyes were sharp-watching her, studying her.

Miranda hesitated, he was noticing. Too much.

She needed to steer this away, to shift his focus before he started asking the wrong questions.

"It's nothing," she said, forcing a small smile. "I promise."

Nick exhaled, rubbing the back of his neck. He still looked uncertain but nodded.

"If it's nothing, then eat something," he said. "You skipped breakfast."

Relieved that he was letting it go, Miranda let out a weak laugh.

"Fine," she relented, moving toward the fridge.

Nick watched her for a beat longer, then finally picked up his coffee again.

She turned her back to him, pretending to rummage through the fridge-but inside, her heart was racing.

The nausea hit fast.

One second, Miranda was still rummaging through the fridge, willing herself to push through the queasiness, the next—a violent churn tore through her gut, and she knew she wasn't going to stop it this time.

She barely made it down the hall before she lunged into the bathroom, dropping to her knees just in time.

Nick was right behind her.

"Miranda!" His voice was sharp with concern, but she couldn't answer-not when her entire body was rebelling against her.

She braced herself against the toilet, squeezing her eyes shut as another wave crashed over her.

Nick hovered in the doorway, his footsteps hesitant before he crouched beside her.

"You're definitely not fine." His voice was low, but there was no missing the frustration layered beneath it.

Miranda wiped the back of her hand across her mouth, forcing herself to breathe.

"I told you," she rasped, "just something I ate."

Nick's jaw clenched. "Don't do that."

She blinked up at him, still feeling unsteady. "Do what?"

"Lie to me."

The words hung between them.

Nick sat back on his heels, arms resting on his knees as he studied her. Really studied her.

She could feel his mind working, fitting together all the little signs she had tried too hard to ignore-the fatigue, the changes in her appetite, the way she'd been avoiding him in quiet, subtle ways.

"Miranda," he said, his voice softer this time, "something's going on."

She wanted to tell him. To lean into him, let him put the pieces together instead of fighting to keep them apart.

But the fear was still there.

Her fingers trembled as she gripped the counter and forced herself to look at him. She was done running from this.

"Nick," she whispered, her voice shaking. "I'm pregnant."

Silence.

Nick didn't move, didn't blink—just stared at her, as if he hadn't heard her right.

Miranda swallowed hard, her breath unsteady. "I should have told you sooner. I—I was scared. But you deserve to know."

Nick let out a slow breath, his expression unreadable. Then, finally, he spoke. "You're... pregnant?"

Miranda nodded, her heart hammering in her chest.

Nick exhaled sharply, rubbing a hand over his face before looking at her again. This time, something shifted in his eyes—something raw and uncertain, but real.

Miranda," he whispered, voice barely above a breath. "We're having a baby?"

Tears burned at the corners of her eyes. "We are."

His breath left him in a slow exhale. He stared at her, searching for something—understanding, maybe, or a connection that still felt just out of reach.

Then, finally, he nodded.

"I—I want to be happy," he admitted, his voice rough. "I feel like I should be. But—" He swallowed hard, his fingers twitching at his sides. "I still don't remember everything, Miranda."

Her heart clenched as a tear fell down her cheek. She had known this moment would be hard, but hearing him say it still stung.

"I know," she whispered.

Nick ran a hand down his face, exhaling sharply. "I don't want to say the wrong thing. I don't want to feel like this is something happening to someone else." He shook his head. "But I'm trying. I swear, I'm trying."

Miranda stepped closer, reaching for his hand. He hesitated for only a second before letting her take it.

"I don't need you to have all the answers, Nick," she said gently. "I just need you here."

Nick let out a slow, shuddering breath. Then he squeezed her hand. "I am here."

And for now, that was enough.

25

Miranda traced the rim of her mug, her gaze locked on the small box sitting on the kitchen table. It was just like the last one—plain, no return address, no postage. As if it had simply appeared.

The pendant light above her flickered softly, casting long shadows across the countertops. Outside, the last blush of dusk had long faded into quiet, creeping dark. The box's corners were damp, like it had been left outside just long enough to gather dew.

She hadn't heard a knock. No car had pulled up. Nothing.

The sight of it twisted something in her gut.

She glanced toward the living room, where Nick sat flipping through a woodworking catalog, fingers absently rubbing the scar on his temple. He looked normal, at ease. But something in his posture—the set of his shoulders, the way his foot tapped the floor—told her he wasn't as relaxed as he wanted to seem.

Their conversation from the night before still hovered in the space between them.

Telling him about the baby had been a relief... but it hadn't solved everything.

He held her hand, promised he was trying—but the distance between them was still there, quiet and hollow.

And now, this.

She reached out, fingers hesitant. The box wasn't sealed. Just folded closed. No tape. No label.

Miranda lifted the lid.

Inside, an envelope.

Her stomach dropped.

She opened it with slow, shaking hands.

The first photo slipped into her palm—grainy, black-and-white. Her and Arthur. Smiling. An engagement party from long ago, chandeliers glowing above them like frozen stars.

Behind it, tucked inside a vintage Christmas card, was another photo.

This one was worse.

It was their cottage.

Now.

Miranda's pulse kicked hard beneath her skin.

The angle of the photo was unmistakable—taken from the trees that lined the edge of their backyard.

She stared at it, her lungs tightening as if the air had grown thinner.

Her fingers dug into the envelope as she pulled out the card.

"Christmas is about remembering the past... and sometimes, about unfinished business."

The handwriting was sharp. Controlled. Not Arthur's.

Arthur was gone.

So who sent this?

She slammed the envelope shut just as Nick walked in, stretching with a tired sigh.

"You coming to bed?" he asked, rubbing a hand over his beard.

Miranda blinked at him, her voice catching only slightly. "Yeah. Just... needed a minute."

Nick crossed the kitchen, grabbing a glass from the cupboard and filling it at the sink. "That's been happening a lot lately."

She shrugged, tucking her hands into her sleeves. "My mind won't shut off."

He nodded but didn't look at her. "Same here. It's like... my brain's running a race I never signed up for."

Her chest ached at the gentleness in his voice, the way it cut through the space between them without demanding anything.

He watched her for a moment, something unreadable flickering in his expression. Then he held out a hand—quiet, tentative.

"Come to bed with me?"

She nodded and slipped her fingers into his. His grip was warm, careful—like he was still trying to understand where they stood.

As they walked toward the hallway, he tugged her gently into his side. She leaned against him, letting herself breathe.

He pressed a soft kiss to her temple, and she felt the effort behind it—not forced, just... deliberate. A kindness from someone who didn't remember everything, but still wanted to show her he cared.

"C'mon," he said. "Let's try to sleep."

But as he led her away, Miranda glanced back at the drawer.

The envelope was hidden. But it hadn't gone anywhere.

26

After last night, Miranda hadn't been able to sleep. She'd spent the hours staring at the ceiling, exhaustion pressing down but never pulling her under.

Nick hadn't spoken to her at all this morning. She heard him moving in the kitchen about half an hour ago—the clink of a mug, the soft groan of the cabinet hinge—but not a single word between them.

It wasn't like him.

At least, not lately.

Things had been better. Not perfect, but better. He'd been present. Talking. Reaching for her again in quiet ways. But something about this morning felt different. Off.

No more waiting. No more excuses. She had to tell him now.

She stepped into the kitchen and saw him standing by the window, a cup of coffee cradled in his hands. His posture was tense, shoulders tight and unmoving. The rich scent of coffee hung heavy in the air, but it didn't mask the chill that had crept into the space between them.

For a moment, she hesitated.

He hadn't noticed her yet, but the distance between them felt wide—like something had already racked open before she even spoke a word.

"Nick.'

He didn't turn at first.

Then he exhaled slowly and looked at her. He looked exhausted—not just physically, but down to the soul. She recognized that expression. The one that said, *I'm trying to hold it together, but I'm slipping.*

"I'm sorry it's taken me this long to open up," she said, her voice quiet. "But I need to tell you something."

He studied her, silent.

She swallowed hard, bracing herself. "Someone's been leaving photos. Of me. From... a long time ago. At first I thought they were nothing, but another came in yesterday."

Nick's fingers tightened around his mug before he set it down—too carefully. His jaw flexed, and his exhale was sharp through his nose.

When she reached into the drawer and pulled out the envelope, he didn't take it. His eyes locked on hers instead, unreadable.

"Someone's been watching you," he said, voice low and tight.

"Yes."

Silence stretched between them.

Then something shifted in Nick's expression.

"That night," he murmured. "The figure I saw in the garden."

"I remember," Miranda said quietly. "You did."

"But you didn't say anything," he continued, voice fraying. "Not after. Not when the photos started. You didn't connect the dots with me. You just—" He wreaked a hand through his hair. "You kept it to yourself."

She took a shaky breath. "I wasn't sure at first. And then I thought maybe... maybe it would stop. That it wasn't worth dragging you into if it turned out to be nothing."

He turned on her, not angry but overwhelmed. "Miranda, I *saw* someone outside our house. You knew that. You *knew*, and you didn't come back to it. You just let it sit."

"I was trying not to make it worse," she said. "You were healing. You didn't even remember who I was for a while, and this—felt like too much."

Nick let out a sharp exhale, turning away as he pressed his palms flat against the counter.

"I'm not mad you were scared," he said after a moment. "I'm mad you didn't trust me. Not with this."

His voice cracked slightly.

She stepped forward, but he didn't move to meet her.

"I needed you to tell me," he continued. "Not after the second photo. Not after it got worse. From the beginning. I may not have all my memories, but I'm not helpless. I *should've known*."

Miranda's throat tightened. "I know. You're right."

He looked at her then—really looked—and the hurt behind his eyes nearly knocked the breath out of her.

"I just need a minute," he muttered, turning toward the door.

His hand hovered on the knob, his back to her.

"I'll come back," he said. Softer. Still firm. "I just... I need to clear my head."

And then he was gone.

27

Nick had no clue where he was going. He just walked.

His breath came out sharp, his chest tightening as the weight of it all crashed into him. He had been fighting like hell to remember—to piece himself back together. And the whole time, she had been standing right there, watching him drown, saying nothing.

The betrayal hit harder than he expected.

Was it betrayal?

Or was it just fear?

Nick scrubbed a hand down his face as he walked, barely noticing the street lights flickering on as the sun dipped below the horizon. His hands were still shaking.

He had told himself that the worst part of this whole mess was the memory loss—that not knowing his own life was the thing tearing him apart.

But this?

This was worse.

She hadn't told him someone was watching her. Someone had been following her, leaving pictures, creeping into their life like a shadow—and she had kept it from him.

He should have known. She should have trusted him enough to tell him.

His fingers curled into fists, his boots hitting the pavement harder now as frustration burned in his chest. He wasn't mad that she had wanted to protect him. He was mad that she didn't trust him enough to let him

For weeks, he had felt like a stranger in his own life. In his own body. But this was his life. His wife.

And he had been the last to know.

Nick barely registered the hotel sign glowing ahead of him until he found himself in front of it, staring up at the flickering VACANCY light like it might have the answers he needed.

He could check in. Stay the night. Let his mind settle.

Taking a deep breath, he moved toward the hotel entrance, the automatic doors sliding open with a gentle hum. The lobby was quiet, dimly lit, and uninviting, perfectly matching his mood. He approached the front desk, quickly completed the check-in process, and accepted the key card with a silent nod.

Miranda stood motionless in the heavy silence that followed Nick's abrupt exit, the echo of the slammed door still ringing painfully in her ears. The emptiness of the kitchen pressed against her, suffocating, almost unbearable.

Hours had passed, yet she still hadn't moved from the spot near the counter, replaying their confrontation over and over again in her mind. The truth came too late and instead of protecting him like she had hoped, she pushed him away.

Please help me, Lord. I don't know how to fix this. I've made mistakes—I've hurt him. (A shaky breath.) But You brought us together for a reason. Please, soften his heart. Let him hear me, wherever he is. Bring him back to me.

As Miranda spoke, her voice broke with genuine heartbreak. "Nick, I'm sorry. Please come back to me." The words weren't just spoken—they poured directly from her soul, raw and filled with longing.

As Nick reached for the door handle, a sharp, gut-deep pull yanked him back.

Not physically. Not in any way he could see. But in a way he felt.

The hairs on the back of his neck stood up, a cold shiver rolling down his spine. He squeezed his eyes shut, bracing himself against the sensation, but it didn't fade.

If anything, it deepened.

Her. Miranda.

Nick's fingers clenched around the handle as a sudden wave of emotion hit him.

She was hurting. He felt it.

Not just an assumption. Not just a guess. It was real. Palpable. Like something tethered them together, stretching between them even now, pulling him home.

His chest rose, then paused mid-motion, suspended in silence.

And then, like a whisper in the back of his mind, he heard her.

I'm sorry Nick. Come back to me.

Nick exhaled sharply, shaking his head as he turned away from the room door.

He didn't know what this was—why he felt her like this—but he knew one thing for sure. He couldn't leave her.

And more than that—

He didn't want to.

When he finally reached the familiar porch, Nick paused, breath uneven. The house was dark and quiet, but his heart still felt Miranda's sorrow as strongly as if it were his own. He took a shaky breath, steeling himself as he placed his hand on the doorknob. The memory lingered, gentle but unyielding, reminding him that he belonged nowhere else but with her.

He pushed the door open quietly, stepping inside and ready to face whatever came next.

Miranda lay quietly in bed, eyes closed though sleep continued to elude her. The gentle weight and warmth of Tinsel curled beside her, pressed protectively against her stomach, purring softly. Somehow, the little cat seemed to know—cats always knew these things. Miranda took comfort in Tinsel's quiet presence, her hand resting gently on the cat's soft fur as if drawing strength from her tiny companion.

Suddenly, she heard the front door open, the familiar creak echoing faintly through the silent house. Her heart jumped, hope and anxiety swirling within her as footsteps moved cautiously down the hall. She held her breath, afraid to move, afraid to hope too much.

The bedroom door eased open slowly, and there stood Nick, his silhouette outlined by the dim hallway light. Miranda opened her eyes, meeting his hesitant gaze as he stood in the doorway, looking at her with uncertainty but also something deeper—regret, longing, perhaps even relief.

"Nick," she whispered softly, unable to hide the tremble in her voice.

He took a careful step into the room, eyes locking onto her face, before drifting to Tinsel curled protectively against her abdomen. A flicker of warmth crossed his expression, quickly followed by vulnerability and uncertainty.

"Miranda," he said softly, stepping closer, the tension easing just slightly from his shoulders. "Can we talk?"

Miranda swallowed, sitting up slightly as she watched Nick step further into the room.

"Yeah," she whispered, her fingers curling instinctively into the blanket. "We can talk."

Nick hesitated just a second before crossing the room. He didn't sit on the bed, not yet, but he moved to the chair beside it, resting his elbows on his knees.

Up close, she could see it.

The exhaustion beneath his eyes. The tension in his jaw. The way his fingers tapped restlessly against each other—a tell she knew all too well.

He was trying to find the right words.

She didn't rush him.

Finally, Nick exhaled. "I don't know how to do this, Miranda."

Her breath tangled in her chest.

He wasn't meeting her eyes, just staring at his hands. Like he was still bracing himself for something.

"I don't know how to just... forget everything that's happened. How to move past the things you kept from me," he admitted, his voice tight.

Miranda swallowed hard, her throat feeling raw from so much that had already been said, and even more that hadn't.

"I don't expect you to forget," she said softly.

Nick's head finally lifted, his eyes searching hers.

"You should've told me, Miranda." His voice wasn't sharp—just tired. "From the very beginning."

"I know," she admitted. "I should have."

Nick ran a hand down his face, exhaling through his nose. "And the pictures... everything about them makes my skin crawl. Whoever this is, they're playing a long game. And I can't shake the feeling that me being in the dark about it was exactly what they wanted."

Miranda stiffened.

Nick caught the movement, his gaze sharpening.

"You think the timing was intentional?" she asked hesitantly.

Nick nodded. "I do. That first photo showing up right after I got home?" He shook his head. "That wasn't a coincidence. It was calculated. Maybe they were testing me, seeing what I remembered. Or maybe..." His voice dropped slightly. "Maybe they were waiting for you to be just vulnerable enough to break."

Miranda pressed a hand to her temple, overwhelmed by the implications.

"So what do we do?" she asked, voice small.

Nick leaned forward slightly, resting his forearms on his knees. "First, we don't let them control us with fear. That's what they want. And second..."

He hesitated, like he was weighing the next words carefully.

"We handle this together," he finally said.

Miranda's breath caught.

Together.

She had wanted to hear those words for so long, but now that she had, she barely knew how to respond.

Nick rubbed the back of his neck. "It doesn't mean I've figured everything out yet. I haven't. I'm still mad. I still don't know how to trust you the way I used to."

Miranda's stomach twisted, but she nodded, bracing herself for the truth.

"But," he continued, his voice softer now, "I know that leaving didn't fix anything. And staying away from you didn't make me feel any less... tied to you. I don't think it ever could."

Miranda swallowed back the lump in her throat. "Nick, I—"

"I don't need promises," he interrupted gently. "I just need you to mean it when you say we're in this together."

A tear slipped down Miranda's cheek, and she quickly wiped it away.

She had spent so long fighting to protect him, only to realize he had been protecting her this whole time, too.

And she didn't want to fight against him anymore.

She wanted to fight with him.

"I do," she whispered. "I mean it."

Nick's shoulders relaxed—just slightly, just enough.

And for the first time in weeks, they sat in the same space without a chasm between them.

28

The last couple of days had been better. Not perfect—just better. Not the way things used to be. Not whole. But better.

Nick had been present. Not just physically, but in a way he hadn't been since the accident.

They had talked—really talked. Not just about the past, but about the future.

They still had a long way to go, but for the first time, Miranda let herself believe that they could find their way back to each other.

So when the nausea started creeping in earlier than usual that morning, Miranda didn't panic.

She'd felt off all week—sluggish, achy, like her body was always one step behind her—but she chalked it up to stress, hormones, maybe even the weather. Midwives weren't immune to rough pregnancies. She knew that. She'd warned enough women about the ebb and flow of symptoms.

But now... now it was something else.

She was kneeling on the bathroom floor, one arm draped over the toilet bowl, forehead pressed against the cool porcelain. Her skin felt clammy. Her fingers tingled. She was shaking, not from effort—but from weakness.

This wasn't just a bad morning.

She heard Nick's footsteps before he spoke. "Miranda?"

She opened her mouth, but the answer came out hoarse. "I'm okay."

Liar.

She wasn't even sure who she was trying to convince—him, or herself.

The door creaked open.

Nick stepped inside, taking one look at her pale face and trembling body before crouching beside her.

"I'm calling Dr. Patel," he said firmly.

"Nick—" she groaned.

"No. You've been throwing up for days. You're not keeping anything down. You can barely stand." His voice didn't rise, but it cut through the fog in her brain like a chisel. "You're dehydrated. You need help."

She closed her eyes. "I didn't think it would get this bad."

"I know," he said gently. "But it did."

A soft chirp echoed from the hallway. Tinsel padded into the room, her fur fluffed, tail flicking with quiet judgment.

Nick glanced at her. "See? Even the cat's backing me up."

Miranda managed a weak laugh, then leaned into his shoulder as he wrapped an arm around her.

Nick helped her to her feet, his touch firm but careful—like he wasn't sure how close he was allowed to be. He didn't speak much as they walked to the bedroom, his arm braced around her just enough to steady her, not enough to linger.

When they reached the bed, he paused, then pulled back slightly, giving her space. "You okay to sit?"

She nodded. "Yeah."

He waited until she lowered herself onto the edge of the bed before removing her slippers. His movements were efficient, quiet. Like he was helping a stranger out of obligation, not a wife he had once adored.

But she didn't blame him. Not really.

"Do you want something cooler to wear?" he asked, still not quite looking at her.

She swallowed. "If you don't mind grabbing a t-shirt."

He nodded once, retreating to her dresser. After a second of hesitation, his hand brushed over a few options before settling on a soft, worn blue t-shirt.

He stared at it for a beat, like he wasn't sure why he'd picked it.

"Here," he said, handing it to her without meeting her eyes. "This... looked comfortable."

Miranda's fingers closed around the fabric. It was the one she always wore when she didn't feel well—he couldn't possibly know that.

Unless... some part of him did.

She said nothing, just nodded as he turned to give her privacy.

That small gesture of privacy—the old Nick would have stayed, teasing her gently, tucking her hair behind her ear.

But this version... this version was still lost.

Once she was settled against the pillows, he came back with a small cup of water, handing it to her without sitting.

She sipped carefully, the cold ice was a relief. "Thanks." In her head she wondered how long it would be until this also came back up.

Nick lingered awkwardly at the edge of the room, his hands shoved in his pockets again. She could tell he wanted to do something—say something—but couldn't figure out what.

"I didn't want to worry you," she said after a moment. Her voice was quiet, almost tired.

He gave a short, humorless breath. "Bit late for that."

She looked up. "I know. I just... I thought it would pass."

He nodded once, staring at a spot on the floor. "It's not like I have a lot to compare it to, but this doesn't look normal."

She let out a soft, almost bitter laugh. "It's not."

That pulled his gaze to her, something flickering behind his eyes. Worry. Frustration. Maybe even fear.

"You've been taking care of me since the accident," he said slowly, like he was choosing every word with care. "I didn't realize it was costing you this much."

"It's not your fault."

"I didn't say it was."

Silence settled between them, heavy and complicated. She wanted to reach for his hand, but she didn't. She wasn't sure he'd let her.

Instead, she folded her arms around her stomach, pressing her palm gently into the warmth there.

"I didn't expect to feel this weak so soon," she admitted. "I can usually push through things. I've helped women in labor with fevers and vomiting and even passing out. I thought I could handle it."

Nick crossed his arms, finally leaning his weight against the doorframe. "But this isn't someone else. It's you."

The words surprised them both.

Miranda swallowed. "Yeah."

He looked at her like he was trying to read a language he used to know. Like the answers were there, just out of reach. "Dr. Patel will be here soon."

She nodded. "Good."

Another beat of silence passed before he said, "I'll go wait for her outside. Let her know she can come straight in."

He pushed away from the wall, but before he turned to leave, his eyes lingered on her face.

"Miranda... if there's more going on than you're saying..."

She met his gaze, not blinking. "There is."

Something in his expression faltered. But he didn't press her—not yet. He just nodded once and walked out.

Tinsel hopped up onto the bed and made her way to her usual perch.

29

Nick stood at the edge of the porch, hands stuffed in his jacket pockets, watching the gravel road with more focus than necessary.

She parked and stepped out with her usual calm efficiency, a canvas medical bag slung over her shoulder and a look that said she wasn't in the mood for small talk. She didn't need to be. Her presence alone was steadying.

"Hey," she greeted, giving Nick a once-over. "You holding up?"

He nodded, then shook his head. "I don't know. She's been sick for a few days—nausea, exhaustion—but this morning it got worse. She's keeping less down than usual, and she looks... worn out."

Anaya approached with a measured pace. "Sounds like it finally caught up to her."

"I think she didn't want me to see how bad it was," he said, voice low. "Or maybe she didn't want to admit it."

"That tracks." She adjusted the strap on her bag. "Pregnant midwives are the worst patients. Too much pride, too much knowledge."

Nick gave a short, barely-there smile.

"She's in bed?" Anaya asked, heading for the porch steps.

"Yeah," he replied, following her to the door. "First room on the right."

Anaya paused before going in. "You coming?"

Nick hesitated. "I will. Just give me a minute."

She studied him for a moment—quiet, sharp, but not unkind. Then she nodded. "Alright. I'll check her over first."

Nick held the door for her, then lingered just outside, letting the cool air settle over his skin as the door clicked shut behind her.

The front door opened and closed with a click.

Miranda heard it from the bedroom, her eyes half-lidded against the late afternoon light filtering through the curtains. Footsteps followed—measure, purposeful—crossing the hardwood floor and moving steadily toward her door.

She didn't need to look to know it was Anaya.

A gentle knock came next, barely a formality, followed by the creak of the door as it swung open.

"Why didn't you call sooner?"

Anaya stood in the doorway, her coat still on and her medical bag looped over one arm. Her sharp eyes swept over Miranda without a hint of pretense.

Miranda tried to push herself upright but gave up halfway. "I thought it would pass."

Anaya walked in and set her bag on the dresser with a soft thud. "You're a midwife. You know better than to ignore the signs like this."

"I didn't ignore them," Miranda said, her voice barely above a whisper. "I just... didn't expect it to get this bad."

Anaya turned to face her, arms crossed now, but not unkind. "That's exactly the kind of thinking that gets people in trouble."

"I thought I could manage. I've just been focused on everything else."

"Well you thought wrong." She sighed and softened the edge in her tone. "But I get it. You're used to being the one who takes care of everyone else."

Miranda's eyes fluttered shut. "It's hard to admit I need help."

"Well, good news," Anaya said, pulling on a pair of gloves. "You don't have to. I'm here."

She moved to the bedside and gently took Miranda's wrist, checking her pulse. "You're pale. Clammy. You've probably been dehydrated for a couple days, and your energy's tanking because of it."

"I haven't kept anything down since last night."

"You should've called me sooner."

"I didn't want to make it a thing."

"It's too late for that," Anaya said, not harshly—just honest. "It's okay to let someone else carry the weight for a while."

Miranda exhaled slowly. "I'm scared Anaya."

That was all she had left.

The tears pricked her eyes, but she didn't try to explain. She was too tired—too worn down to untangle the thoughts spinning through her head. The nausea, the weight of the baby growing inside her, the ache of watching Nick drift farther away—it was all too much.

Anaya didn't press her.

She just gave a small nod, then moved with quiet purpose to open her bag. "Alright," she said gently. "No more questions. Let's just get you feeling like yourself again."

Miranda let her eyes drift shut.

She heard the crinkle of packaging, the soft clink of glass, the hum of something steady returning. It was oddly comforting—the rhythm of Anaya's movements, her calm efficiency, her silence.

The door creaked a moment later.

Nick stepped in.

He hesitated, taking in the scene: Miranda lying pale against the pillows, Anaya focused beside her, the quiet hiss of fluid being drawn into a syringe.

"She okay?" he asked quietly.

Anaya didn't look up. "Dehydrated, drained, and stubborn as ever."

Nick stepped closer. "Is she asleep?"

"She's listening," Anaya said. "Just too wiped to chime in."

Miranda didn't open her eyes, but her lips twitched—just barely.

Anaya found a vein on the first try and slid the IV into place with steady hands. "Fluids should help. Give her system a boost. But she needs rest. Real rest."

Nick pulled the chair up beside the bed, close but not too close.

Miranda felt the shift in the room when he sat—like the air settled differently with him there.

She didn't speak. Neither did he.

And for now, that was enough.

The soft drip of the IV filled the room. Anaya adjusted the flow, checked the tubing, then moved back to her bag. Nick stayed seated, eyes on Miranda, elbows braced on his knees.

After a few minutes, Anaya looked over at her. Miranda's breathing had evened out, her lashes resting still against her cheek.

"She's out," Anaya murmured. "Good."

Nick nodded, but his gaze didn't move.

Anaya dropped her voice further, gathering supplies with a quiet efficiency. "You okay?"

He exhaled through his nose. "No. Not really."

She glanced over her shoulder. "You want to elaborate, or are we just naming emotions today?"

Nick gave a tired huff of air that might've been a laugh. "I don't know how to be who she needs me to be."

"She doesn't need you to be anything but here."

"That doesn't feel like enough."

Anaya turned and leaned against the dresser, arms crossed, voice calm. "You're not the only one who's lost something, Nick. This is hard for her too. Probably harder."

"I can see that." He scrubbed a hand over his face. "Even when she doesn't say it."

He looked over at the bed. "She keeps reaching for something in me I don't remember how to give. It's like I'm... I don't know. A placeholder. Standing in for a version of me she still believes is coming back."

Anaya didn't rush to respond.

"Well," she finally said, "maybe that version of you is still in there. You just haven't bumped into him again yet."

Nick's mouth twisted like he wasn't sure if that was comforting or not. "She deserves better than half a husband."

"She's not asking for perfect, Nick. She's asking for effort. And I think you're giving more than you realize."

Nick looked at Miranda again. Her face was turned slightly toward them, eyes closed, breath even.

"She doesn't know I'm scared too," he said softly.

Anaya's gaze lingered on him. "She knows."

Neither of them noticed the slight shimmer of tears forming at the corners of Miranda's eyes.

She stayed still. Silent.

But this time, the warmth in her chest didn't come from the IV drip.

It came from the truth she wasn't meant to hear.

She held onto it as her body relaxed, the weight of exhaustion finally tipping her over the edge. Her breathing slowed, her hand loosened where it had been clutching the blanket, and her thoughts faded with the steady rhythm of the drip.

By the time Nick looked at her again, she was fast asleep.

And for the first time in days... she looked at peace.

30

Nick woke up before Miranda for once.

That alone was unusual.

For the first time in days, he didn't hear her rushing to the bathroom or stirring restlessly. The house was quiet—peaceful, even. The kind of quiet that didn't feel empty... just calm.

He rolled onto his side, blinking at the sight of Miranda still curled up in bed, her breathing soft and steady. The color had returned to her cheeks, just a hint, but it was enough to ease something that had been twisted up tight in his chest.

And, of course, Tinsel was right there, curled protectively at her side, one fluffy paw resting squarely over Miranda's belly like she'd appointed herself guardian of all things sacred.

Nick's lips tugged into a faint smile. "Glad to see your patient survived the night, Nurse Tinsel."

The cat didn't even blink. Just purred louder, her body practically humming with smug satisfaction.

Nick sat up, stretching slowly. His shoulders ached from the tension he'd been carrying for days, but the sight of Miranda still resting—really resting—made it easier to breathe.

She was okay.

And that was all that mattered.

Across the bed, Miranda stirred. Her fingers shifted beneath the blanket, then drifted instinctively to her belly. She didn't open her eyes, not yet—but she smiled softly as her palm settled just over the place where Tinsel's paw still rested.

Thank you for today, she thought. *For rest. For another chance.*

She didn't know what today would bring, but for now, there was breath in her lungs, warmth at her side, and a strange, quiet hope blooming inside her.

By mid-morning, Miranda was awake and propped up against a pile of pillows, slowly sipping water between small bites of toast. Her movements were sluggish, but her color was better, and the sharp edge of exhaustion had finally begun to fade.

Nick hovered, quietly pleased, making sure she had what she needed without saying too much.

Just as she finished her toast, a knock sounded at the door.

"I've got it," Nick said, already standing.

"I can walk," Miranda offered, though she made no move to get up.

"You can sit," he corrected, shooting her a look over his shoulder.

Tinsel chirped in agreement from her spot on the pillow.

Miranda rolled her eyes but didn't argue.

Nick opened the door to find Anaya standing there, medical bag in hand—and beside her, Lydia.

"Long time no see, Mr. Owens," Lydia said with a bright grin.

Nick arched a brow. "You brought backup?"

Dry amusement colored her voice. "I figured if I came alone, your wife might try to convince me she was ready to run a marathon," Anaya replied. "Lydia's good at talking sense into stubborn pregnant women."

Lydia grinned. "Figured I'd get a head start. We'll be seeing a lot of each other soon enough."

Nick stepped back to let them in. "Well, she's not running any marathons today. Doctor's orders."

When Miranda saw them walk into the bedroom together, she groaned dramatically. "Oh no. Not both of you."

Anaya set down her bag with a smirk. "You didn't tell me you were running on fumes for a *week*, so I figured I was allowed to bring reinforcements."

Lydia perched on the edge of the bed. "How's our mama doing this morning?"

Miranda leaned her head back against the pillows. "Much better. But this little intervention makes me think I should pretend I'm still sick, just to make it worth your time."

"Don't even joke," Lydia said, nudging her knee. "You scared people."

Anaya pulled out her stethoscope. "Sit up a little straighter, let's see how much progress Nick's hovering actually accomplished."

Nick leaned against the doorway, arms crossed. "Hey. My hovering is top-tier, thank you very much."

Miranda smiled faintly. "That it is."

As Anaya listened to her chest, Lydia gently checked the IV site. "No swelling, no irritation. Fluids are doing their job."

Anaya checked Miranda's pulse, then pressed the back of her hand to her forehead. "Still a little weak. But better. You don't look like someone who could collapse mid-sentence anymore."

Miranda looked at Nick. "Told you I was fine."

"You're better," Anaya corrected. "There's a difference."

Nick dipped his head with a soft smile. "Still. Thank you."

Anaya clipped a small pulse oximeter to Miradna's finger. "I want you on fluids one more day, just to be safe. Then we'll reassess."

Miranda groaned. "So, house arrest continues."

"Bed rest," Lydia corrected. "Not a prison sentence."

Miranda muttered," Feels like one."

Anaya raised a brow. "If you keep pushing, I'll promote Tinsel to parole officer."

Miranda snorted. "She already thinks she runs the house."

Tinsel stretched dramatically at the mention of her name, her purr rumbling like thunder.

Nick chuckled. "Yeah, I'm pretty sure she does run the house."

Once the check-up was done, Anaya packed her things. "She's on the mend. Keep her resting, keep her hydrated."

Nick nodded, his hand resting lightly over Miranda's. "Got it."

"I'll stop by again tomorrow," Anaya said. "Unless she gets any wild ideas about going for a hike."

Lydia stood and pointed at Miranda with a teasing glare. "Don't tempt me into dragging you back to the clinic for a lecture on self-care."

Miranda rolled her eyes, but her smile lingered. "You're all bossier than I remember."

Nick squeezed her hand gently. "That's because you're finally sitting still long enough to notice."

Once Anaya and Lydia left, the house settled into a hush again.

Nick paused in the hallway, staring at the quiet door before slowly stepping back inside.

Miranda hadn't moved much. She was still resting against the pillows, IV line gently dripping beside her, Tinsel curled along her hip like a purring shadow. Her eyes were open now, watching him.

He hovered near the dresser, uncertain. "You need anything?"

She shook her head. "No. Just... tired."

He nodded, then crossed the room and pulled the chair closer to her side.

"I didn't sleep much last night," he said. "I kept waking up, checking if you were still breathing."

Her brow lifted faintly. "Not dramatic at all."

He smiled at that. Small, but real.

"I'm trying," he said after a pause, his voice quieter now. "To be here. With you. Even when it's hard."

Miranda looked down at her hands. "It hasn't been easy for either of us."

"No," he agreed. "But yesterday... I saw how close we came to something worse."

He leaned forward slightly, elbows on his knees. "I know I've felt distant. Like I'm trying to be someone you remember, but I don't always know how. But watching you yesterday—it made me want to stop reaching for memories and just... reach for you."

Miranda's throat tightened, the air suddenly too full.

She didn't answer right away. She just lifted her hand, slowly, and let it drift into his.

Their fingers laced without effort.

Nick looked at their joined hands for a long moment before glancing back at her.

"I don't want to be a stranger anymore."

"You're not," she whispered.

And for the first time in what felt like forever, the silence between them didn't ache.

It rested.

Somewhere between his steady breathing and the warmth of her hand in his, Miranda let herself drift again—this time not from exhaustion, but comfort.

31

Miranda was still resting in the bedroom, just as Anaya and Lydia had instructed that morning. Their visit put Nick at ease—at least enough to stop hovering.

Nick wasn't convinced Miranda would fully listen to the "rest" part, but for now, she was bundled up in bed, her only company being Tinsel, who had taken up residence at her feet like a tiny, furry guard. Or Parole Officer. As Anaya had said.

He had just finished tidying up the kitchen when he heard the knock.

It wasn't urgent. Not forceful, not timid—just ... casual.

Nick frowned. They weren't expecting anyone.

Wiping his hands on a dish towel, he made his way to the door. Probably a neighbor. Maybe a package.

When he opened it, the man standing there looked completely unremarkable.

Blond. Neatly dressed. His smile was easy, his posture relaxed—like someone comfortable in his own skin.

"Hey," the man greeted, his tone friendly but confident. "Sorry to bother you—just wondering if Miranda's home?"

Nick blinked, caught slightly off guard.

It wasn't strange for someone to ask for Miranda. She had clients all over town, and plenty of people stopped by looking for her.

But something about the way the man said her name—like he already knew she was here—made Nick hesitate. He didn't recognize him.

Nick leaned against the doorframe, not blocking the doorway yet, just... observing.

"Who's asking?" he said, keeping his voice neutral.

The man's smile didn't falter. Too easy. Too familiar.

"Wyatt Reynolds," he said, sticking out a hand. "Miranda and I go way back."

Nick glanced at the offered handshake but didn't take it.

Not because he was being rude—just because something unsettled him.

That name... Wyatt Reynolds. It didn't ring any bells.

Nick forced his expression to stay neutral. "You an old friend?"

Wyatt chuckled, the sound casual and easy—but there was a strange edge behind it. He slid his hands into his pockets, leaning back slightly, as if enjoying a private joke. "My family and Miranda... we go back. It's funny how some memories refuse to fade. Isn't it?"

Something about the way Wyatt emphasized the word *fade* sent a faint chill down Nick's spine. He nodded slowly, his gaze sharpening almost instinctively. Nothing Wyatt said was outright suspicious. But the tone, the undercurrent of carefully concealed bitterness—it was like a shadow lurking just beneath the surface.

Nick shifted slightly, still not blocking the doorway, but standing straighter.

"She's resting," he said simply. "Long couple of days."

Wyatt nodded a little too knowingly.

"Yeah, I heard she wasn't feeling great."

Nick's gut went rigid. Heard?

Nick's expression didn't change, but something inside him sharpened.

"Really?" he said smoothly. "Who told you that?"

Wyatt's smile didn't slip, but something in his posture shifted—just slightly, but Nick caught it.

"Oh, just some mutual connections," Wyatt said with a carefully nonchalant shrug.

Mutual connections?

Before Nick could press further, a sudden hiss cut through the air.

Tinsel.

The little cat had crept up beside him, her back arched, fur standing on end, ears pinned flat against her head. She let out another low, warning growl, her tail lashing aggressively.

Nick glanced down at her in surprise. Tinsel wasn't the friendliest cat, but she didn't usually react this way.

Wyatt's gaze flickered to the cat, his expression unreadable. "Guess she doesn't like strangers."

Nick didn't respond immediately, instead watching as Tinsel held her ground, her golden eyes locked onto Wyatt with unwavering intensity.

Something twisted in Nick's stomach. Tinsel wasn't just acting territorial.

She was warning him.

Nick exhaled slowly, forcing himself to stay relaxed. "Yeah, she's picky about people."

A flicker of something unreadable crossed Wyatt's face as he stepped back. "No problem. Just tell her I said hello."

Nick watched as he turned and walked away, not closing the door until Wyatt had disappeared down the driveway.

He glanced down at Tinsel, who was still watching the door, tail flicking, the tension in her tiny body still coiled tight.

Nick swallowed, a cold feeling creeping into his chest.

Slowly, he shut the door, locking it behind him.

For a long moment, he just stood there, staring at the door, his instincts still prickling beneath his skin. Something wasn't right. But what?

The house was silent, but the feeling stayed with him, threading itself into his thoughts long after he walked away.

He passed the kitchen, then the hallway, not quite aware of his own footsteps until he reached the bedroom door again.

Miranda was still resting—blankets drawn around her, the IV drip quietly working beside her, Tinsel curled up at her feet like nothing in the world could touch her now.

She turned her head slightly as he walked in. "Hey. Everything okay?"

Nick nodded, but there was a tension in his jaw. He sat down in the chair that was still beside her.

"There was a guy at the door a little while ago," he said. "Asked for you."

Miranda blinked. "Who?"

"His name is Wyatt. Wyatt Reynolds."

The name meant nothing to her.

Her brows drew together. "I don't know anyone by that name."

Nick studied her face. "He said you go way back. That your families do."

Miranda shook her head slowly. "I've never met anyone named Wyatt Reynolds. I'd remember that."

Nick's frown deepened. "He also said he'd heard you weren't feeling well."

Her stomach turned.

"How?" she whispered.

"He wouldn't say. Just said he had 'mutual connections.' He smiled the whole time, but it felt... fake. Too easy."

Miranda looked away, her thoughts spinning. "I don't like that."

"Tinsel didn't either," Nick said. "She came out of nowhere and hissed at him. I mean really hissed. Back arched. Growling. It was like she saw something that I couldn't."

Miranda's fingers curled around the blanket. Tinsel was still nestled beside her, purring softly, but the unease had crept back into the room like a cold draft.

"Do you think he's been watching us?" she asked quietly.

Nick didn't answer right away. "I don't know."

She closed her eyes for a moment, then opened them again. "I don't feel safe."

Nick leaned forward, reaching for her hand without hesitation this time. "I'm here. I'm not going anywhere."

Miranda gripped his hand tightly, the warmth of it anchoring her even as a chill bloomed in her chest.

She didn't know who Wyatt Reynolds was.

But he clearly knew her.

32

The next few days passed with an uneasy quiet. No further sightings of their strange visitor, no new disturbances—just the echo of lingering unease neither of them could fully shake.

Nick and Miranda did their best to settle back into normalcy, wanting to believe it had all been a fluke. They both hoped life could return to what it had been before, though a quiet tension still lay beneath the surface.

Nick, ever the protective husband, had taken it upon himself to ensure Miranda was actually resting—not that she made it easy. He barely let her leave the bedroom, insisting she needed to recover properly. Every time she so much as shifted to sit up, his watchful gaze followed her like a hawk.

So naturally, when he walked in with a cup of tea and found her sitting up in bed, glasses perched on her nose, fully engrossed in her phone, he stopped in the doorway with a raised brow.

"What are you doing?" he asked, voice laced with suspicion.

"Nothing," Miranda replied far too quickly, though she didn't even glance up.

Nick chuckled, stepping further into the room. "Why don't I believe you?"

"I'm not sure. I'm a very believable person," she said, flashing him an innocent grin.

"Hand me the phone, woman. You are officially cut off." He set the tea on the nightstand and reached for it.

Miranda held onto it stubbornly.

"Miranda."

She huffed, giving him a dramatic look before finally surrendering it. "But I'm so bored. I can't take it anymore. It's not like I'm *working* working. My clients—"

"Are fine. All of your midwife and nurse friends have everything handled," he reminded her, pocketing the phone. "You need to rest."

"But I'm fine, Nick."

He tilted his head again, giving her a knowing look. "The sleep in your eyes says otherwise."

She crossed her arms, pouting. "You're insufferable."

"You married me, so that's kind of on you."

A wry smile tugged at her lips. "You're right. My biggest mistake yet."

Nick grinned, his laughter warm and easy. "I guess I'll go sign the papers. It was nice knowing ya! Now take a nap. I won't take no for an answer."

As much as Miranda fought him on resting, she couldn't deny the comfort of simply being home. Wrapped in her red and white knit blanket, she traced the smooth edge of the vintage snow globe on the nightstand, watching as tiny flecks of white swirled around the miniature Christmas village inside. It wasn't something she thought much about, but its presence was oddly reassuring.

Her gaze drifted toward the bookshelf, where a wooden advent calendar rested, untouched but ever-present. Nick had made it long ago, each tiny drawer meticulously carved with delicate holiday designs—snowflakes, reindeer, toy trains. They never packed it away with the other Christmas decorations. She wasn't even sure why, but it simply felt like it belonged there year-round.

Even now, in early autumn, the quiet remnants of Christmas lingered—not in a loud, celebratory way, but in those small, familiar comforts that neither of them ever quite put away. A set of wooden nutcrackers lined the mantel, a delicate pine wreath hung casually on the coat rack, and the faint scent of cinnamon and clove always seemed to drift through the house, especially when Nick made tea.

It wasn't intentional, but Christmas had a way of staying with them, woven into their lives in a way Miranda never questioned—until now. Sitting here, taking in the small details, she realized how much of their home carried those little touches of warmth and familiarity. How much of it was simply part of them.

She sighed, shifting against the pillows.

Nick had always made places feel like home. Even when she was determined to argue with him about it.

The quiet padding of footsteps pulled her from her thoughts. She looked up just as Nick walked back in, arms crossed as he leaned against the doorway.

"You look deep in thought," he observed.

She smiled softly. "Just thinking about how much of Christmas we keep around, even when we don't mean to."

Nick raised an eyebrow, glancing around. "I guess we do, huh?" He exhaled, shaking his head with amusement. "What can I say? I like warm spaces."

Miranda's smile widened, her fingers absently toying with the blanket. "I think you make them."

Nick looked at her then, something unreadable flickering in his gaze before he stepped forward and sat beside her on the bed. He picked up the snow globe, turning it over in his hands before setting it back down.

"Well," he murmured, "I guess that means you're stuck with me."

Miranda let out a soft laugh, leaning into his side. "Wouldn't have it any other way."

His hand found hers, their fingers lacing together without thought. There was no distance between them now—only warmth, only the quiet echo of everything they were still rebuilding.

Miranda let her free hand settle gently over her stomach. She didn't feel movement, not yet, but... she felt something. A presence. A promise.

Nick noticed her pause. "What's on your mind?"

She was quiet for a moment, then said, "How different everything feels... but how somehow, it still feels like home."

He didn't speak, just squeezed her hand gently, his thumb brushing over her knuckles.

She shifted slightly, letting out a breath. "I think the baby can feel it too."

He glanced at her, surprised—but not in a bad way. Just caught by the sudden tenderness in her voice.

"The baby seems more settled today," she murmured. "Like it knows that we are okay. At least for now."

Nick looked down at their joined hands, then back at her. "It does have a pretty incredible mom."

Miranda smiled, leaning her head on his shoulder. "And a very overbearing dad."

"Protective," he corrected with a grin.

"Same thing."

He didn't argue.

They sat in comfortable silence, the snow globe still gently swirling beside them, the scent of cinnamon lingering in the air.

And in this moment... all was well.

33

Miranda sat curled up on the couch, a book in her lap, but she wasn't reading. Instead, she closed her eyes briefly, offering a silent prayer for peace—for the strength to navigate everything ahead, for Nick, for their baby, and for the lingering weight of uncertainty that pressed against her heart. She had told herself she'd rest today, let Nick take care of everything, but the longer she sat still, the more restless she became. Her body was tired, yes. But her mind buzzed, thoughts swirling with everything that's been going on. The accident, the photos, Wyatt showing up at the door, and most of all, the baby growing inside her.

Her fingers tapped idly against the blanket draped over her legs. She needed something to do, something grounding, something normal. Normally, prayer was her anchor, the thing that kept her steady when the world felt too big. But today, the words wouldn't come—not in the way she needed them to. So she turned to the next best thing. Baking.

Before she even realized it, she was on her feet, padding toward the kitchen.

The scent of vanilla and cinnamon filled the air as Miranda stood at the counter, measuring flour into a bowl. Baking had always been a source of comfort for her—something simple, something steady. It was muscle memory at this point, the way she sifted, stirred, and rolled the dough into perfect shapes.

She glanced toward the living room, listening for any sign that Nick would come in and scold her for being on her feet. Nothing. Good. She knew he'd insist she go back to resting, but that was impossible. Baking made her feel in control.

Without thinking, she reached for the cookie cutters. A star. A sleigh. A reindeer.

Her fingers hesitated over the last one. She frowned, staring down at the festive shapes she'd chosen without even realizing it. It was September after all.

Her breath caught slightly as she studied them. Why had she picked these? She had a whole collection of cookie cutters—flowers, hearts, even little teacups—but her hands had gone for the Christmas ones first. The ones she always used in December, the ones that filled the house with the scents and shapes of the season.

A strange warmth settled over her. It wasn't the oven, which was still preheating. No, it was something else. A quiet pull toward the familiar, toward a season that had always felt like home.

And then—

A small flicker of awareness pressed against her senses.

Not physical. Not obvious.

But there. A hum beneath her skin, a whisper in the air, like the way the first snowfall always seemed to come when she wasn't expecting it.

Her hand drifted unconsciously to her stomach.

Was that... her? Or...?

She shook off the thought. She was just tired. Overwhelmed. That was all.

She continued on, pressing the cutters into the dough. It didn't matter. Cookies were cookies. And besides, it wasn't like Nick would notice the shapes.

Or so she thought.

"You realize it's not December, right?"

Miranda nearly jumped, spinning to find Nick leaning in the doorway, arms crossed, amusement flickering in his eyes.

She forced a casual shrug. "What, you don't want Christmas cookies in September?"

Nick's lips curved with playful accusation as he stepped closer. "I just think it's funny how you always do this."

"Do what?"

His expression warmed, hand moving instinctively toward the sleigh-shaped cookie. "Bake like it's Christmas when you need comfort."

Miranda's hands stilled on the rolling pin. She swallowed. "I do not."

Nick popped a piece of dough into his mouth, his grin widening, but his voice held a note of surprise. "Uh-huh. You did the same thing after that awful storm last year... And when your favorite coffee shop closed down..." He trailed off for a second, brow furrowing slightly. "And... oh yeah—after we moved into this house." He blinked, the realization settling in. "I... I remember that." His eyes met hers, something shifting in his expression. "You stress-bake, Miranda. And you Christmas-bake."

She narrowed her eyes at him. "Maybe I just like the shapes." But her chest tightened slightly. She had seen that look before—the moment something came back to him. And now, watching his expression change, she knew. Another memory had clicked into place.

Nick snorted. "Sure you do."

His smirk faded slightly as his gaze dropped lower, landing on the soft curve of her stomach. It wasn't visible yet—not really—but they both knew the baby was there, growing, changing everything.

Nick's palm settled lightly against Miranda's stomach, and at the moment his skin met hers, the air shifted.

Not physically—not in any way the human eye could see—but Nick felt it. A whisper of something just beneath the surface. A hum, low and steady, like the distant echo of bells in the snow.

His chest tightened, breath catching as the warmth spread through his palm. Not heat, exactly. More like... recognition.

Miranda stilled beneath his touch, her own fingers twitching slightly. Her heart fluttered, but not from fear—from something deeper.

Neither her, nor Nick were imagining it.

He didn't say anything about the sensation curling through his fingertips, and neither did she. But they both felt it.

For now, neither of them had the words to explain it. Miranda let out a soft breath, surprised at how much calmer she felt. It wasn't just his presence—it was him. The moment his hand rested there, the faint unease she hadn't even realized she was carrying seemed to fade, as if he was anchoring her in the moment. Maybe that was what he'd always done. The moment his hand met her skin, the hum beneath her ribs deepened, steadying. It wasn't just comfort—it was connection. A silent understanding passed between them, unspoken but undeniable. He was here. He was part of this. And somehow, in a way she couldn't explain, so was the baby. Miranda let out a soft breath, closing her eyes for just a second.

Thank you, Lord, for this life. For this gift.

The words came unbidden, whispered in the quiet corners of her heart, a prayer wrapped in gratitude despite the uncertainty ahead.

"Is this helping?" he asked quietly.

Miranda hesitated, then nodded. "Yeah. It is."

Nick exhaled, squeezing her waist lightly before wrapping his arms around her from behind, resting his chin on her shoulder. "Then I won't fight you on it. But at least sit down while they bake, alright?"

She smiled, leaning back into him. "Deal."

But even as she leaned into him, the hum remained—a quiet pulse of something just beyond understanding.

She didn't have all the answers. But for now, standing here with the scent of cinnamon in the air and Nick beside her, she let herself believe.

Maybe things would be okay again.

34

Nick had been cleared to drive again, which was a relief, but Miranda knew he still wasn't fully at ease behind the wheel. He didn't talk about it, but she could tell. The way his grip tightened on the steering wheel, the way he glanced at the rearview mirror a little too often. He wouldn't admit it, not yet, but she knew him too well. He was still finding his footing—just as she was.

The car ride to the clinic was quiet, comfortable in some ways, tense in others. Miranda rested a hand over her stomach, feeling the steady warmth there, a grounding presence. She hadn't told Nick yet, but she'd been feeling something different lately—more than just the usual symptoms of pregnancy. The hum was stronger, more insistent. And every time Nick was near, it settled, like the baby recognized him.

Nick pulled into the parking lot, shifting into park before glancing at her. "You sure you don't want me to come in?"

Miranda hesitated. She had planned to go in alone, but now, sitting here with the steady beat of Nick's fingers drumming on the steering wheel, she realized she didn't want to.

"Actually," she said softly, "I'd like it if you did."

Nick blinked in surprise, then nodded, already unbuckling his seatbelt. "Alright."

Miranda took a steadying breath as she and Nick stepped into her clinic. They exchanged quiet nods with Carol, who looked up from the front desk and offered a gentle smile.

"Dr. Patel will be ready in a few minutes. She asked me to let you know you can wait in your office until then."

"Thanks, Carol." Miranda placed a reassuring hand on her belly, feeling her pulse quicken slightly. After a week of fluids and bedrest, she was grateful to be here again.

Entering her office, Miranda flipped on the soft desk lamp, casting a comfortable golden glow across the room. Nick stood near the doorway, eyes slowly scanning the space as if trying to reacquaint himself with it.

"So, this is your office," he murmured thoughtfully, stepping further inside. He paused by a framed photograph of Miranda holding a newborn, her smile radiant. "Is this one of your patients?"

Miranda nodded, smiling fondly at the memory. "Yes. That's the first baby who was born here when we opened the clinic."

He studied the photo a moment longer before moving on, his eyes landing on a row of neatly organized books lining the shelves. "Did you read all of these?"

"Most of them, yes," she said softly, amused by his curiosity. "Midwifery journals, birthing guides, holistic wellness—there's always something new to learn."

His gaze drifted to a small glass figurine of a mother cradling a child, placed delicately on her desk. He picked it up carefully, turning it over in his hands. "This feels important."

"It is," Miranda agreed quietly. "Your mom gave that to me. It was a gift when I opened this place. She said it reminded her of what I do."

He gently set it down, a subtle emotion playing across his face as he processed the memory she'd shared. "Do you ever feel like it's hard? Being here, doing this job?"

"Sometimes," she admitted softly, leaning against her desk. "But it's worth every difficult moment. There's nothing like seeing a new life come into the world."

Nick moved closer, gently taking her hand. "I wish I remembered more of this part of your life. I feel like I'm missing something special."

"You're here now," Miranda said reassuringly. "That's what matters."

A gentle knock interrupted their conversation, and Anaya peeked her head inside, arching an eyebrow at Miranda. "Alright, enough hiding out in here. Ready to get this show on the road?"

"Ready," Miranda said with a laugh, squeezing Nick's hand briefly before following Anaya to the exam room.

Once settled, Anaya moved swiftly yet warmly through the initial checks, her manner brisk yet comforting. "Vitals look excellent," she noted with satisfaction. "Looks like letting Nick play nurse hasn't completely backfired."

Miranda huffed with a laugh. "He's been relentless. I think he's secretly enjoying bossing me around."

Anaya grinned. "I knew he had it in him. So—how have *you* actually been feeling? And no deflecting this time."

"Much better," Miranda admitted honestly. "Still tired and anxious—but definitely improved."

"Good," Anaya said gently. "Let's take another look at that heartbeat."

Miranda watched closely as the familiar grainy image appeared on the screen. Their baby shifted gently, tiny arms moving slowly.

"There we go," Anaya murmured, focused intently. "Heartbeat is still faster than usual. Nothing overly concerning yet, but worth mentioning. Let's have a listen."

The room filled with the reassuring sound of their child's swift heartbeat. Miranda's eyes met Nick's, and she felt warmth spread through her chest.

As Nick listened, his expression shifted abruptly, eyes distant yet bright, as if seeing something Miranda couldn't. His grip tightened around her hand, and his breath caught in his chest like it was afraid to move. Flashes of memories surged through his mind—a warm, intimate evening at home, Miranda laughing softly as they danced slowly in their kitchen, her eyes full of love and tenderness, and a sense of profound happiness he had nearly forgotten.

Suddenly, another sound gently wove itself into the rhythm—a soft, echoing pulse that harmonized effortlessly with the first. Miranda felt her heart leap, magic tingling warmly beneath her fingertips. Nick blinked rapidly, the memory fading but leaving warmth behind. His eyes widened slightly, awareness fully returning to the present.

Anaya's brow furrowed in confusion as she adjusted the ultrasound probe, searching intently. "This... shouldn't be possible. I'm hearing two heartbeats, but I'm only seeing one baby."

"Could it be interference or an echo?" Nick asked, his voice carefully controlled.

"Not like this," Anaya replied slowly, clearly puzzled. "Echoes don't sound this clear or rhythmically consistent. This genuinely sounds like two separate heartbeats."

Miranda exchanged a quiet look with Nick, feeling the gentle, reassuring magic swirl protectively around her baby.

Anaya sighed softly, reluctantly admitting defeat, though her curiosity lingered. "I don't like mysteries, Miranda, especially not medical ones. But your baby is healthy, and that's the most important thing." She paused, clearly torn between professional curiosity and personal care. "Just promise you'll call immediately if anything feels off."

"I promise," Miranda assured warmly.

Anaya stood, gently squeezing Miranda's shoulder. "You've done well resting this past week, and things are looking much better. I'm comfortable with you returning to work, but slowly—ease yourself back in. And Nick, make sure she listens."

Nick smiled genuinely. "I'll do my best."

Anaya rolled her eyes affectionately. "Good luck with that. And Miranda—I'm serious. Call if you need anything."

"I will," Miranda promised again, smiling gratefully. "Thank you, Anaya."

After Anaya stepped out, Miranda pressed her palm against her abdomen, still feeling that magical warmth. Nick gently leaned close, whispering softly, "This child of ours is certainly something special."

Miranda smiled, comforted by the quiet certainty of his words. "I think you're right."

35

Miranda felt relief wash over her as they left the clinic. Dr. Patel had officially cleared her to gently ease back into work, and the comforting knowledge that the baby was healthy, despite the unusual heartbeat, brought her peace.

Nick started the car and glanced at her, a soft smile warming his features. "Feeling better now?"

"Much better," Miranda said, returning his smile. She relaxed against the seat, hand resting protectively on her belly. "It's reassuring hearing everything's okay."

He hesitated for a brief moment, his eyes thoughtful as he navigated the familiar roads toward home. Finally, he broke the comfortable silence. "Something happened back there during the ultrasound. I had another memory come back."

Miranda felt her pulse quicken slightly, curiosity and hope mingling together. "What did you remember?"

He glanced at her briefly, eyes gentle. "Us, dancing in the kitchen. You were laughing. I remember feeling... happier than I can describe. It felt like an important moment."

Warmth blossomed in Miranda's chest, emotion rising. "It was our first Christmas together," she said softly, her voice thick with memory. "We didn't have much back then—just that tiny house and a crooked tree, remember? But we danced in the kitchen with the lights off, the tree glowing behind us, and I remember thinking there was nowhere else in the world I'd rather be. You were humming some old carol, holding me like I was the most precious thing you'd ever touched. It was the moment I knew I'd found home."

Nick's smile widened slightly, relief evident on his face. He reached over, gently taking her hand, his thumb brushing comfortingly over her knuckles. "These memories keep coming when I least expect them, triggered by moments like today. It's like our baby is guiding me back."

Miranda felt her throat tighten with emotion. She squeezed his hand gently, blinking away happy tears. "I think you're right. This little one has a magic of their own."

They drove on quietly for a while, content in their silence and renewed connection. Miranda leaned her head back, savoring the peaceful moment, grateful for the magic that seemed to continuously swirl protectively around their growing family.

When they pulled into the driveway, the sun had dipped just enough to bathe the porch in golden light. Nick opened Miranda's door for her, steadying her with an instinctive touch at her lower back as they walked inside.

Tinsel was waiting for them, perched on the back of the couch with her tail twitching. The moment Miranda stepped through the doorway, the cat straightened, ears swiveling forward with intensity. Her snowflake-shaped marking shimmered faintly in the fading light.

"Tinsel?" Miranda murmured, pausing.

The cat leapt down in one fluid motion, landing softly on the rug. She padded straight to Miranda, eyes locked onto her belly, then circled her legs once before sitting and staring up with unblinking focus. Miranda could feel it—something new humming just beneath the surface.

Nick noticed it too. "She's doing the staring thing again."

Miranda crouched carefully and reached out, her hand resting over the baby as she watched Tinsel's reaction. The air seemed to hum faintly, almost as if the room itself was holding its breath.

And then—just for a moment—Tinsel purred. Not the usual low rumble of contentment, but a strange, melodic sound, almost musical in tone. Her eyes glowed with a knowing light, and she nudged Miranda's belly gently with her head.

Miranda's brows furrowed slightly. "She only does this when something's... different."

Tinsel hopped onto the windowsill nearby. Her tail flicked once, but her eyes remained fixed on them.

"She knows," Miranda said quietly. "Even if we don't yet."

Nick didn't answer at first. Then he stepped forward and slipped his hand into hers, giving it a soft squeeze. "We'll figure it out."

<h1 style="text-align:center">36</h1>

Miranda had been looking forward to getting back into her routine. She told herself that today would feel normal. She had done this for years—guiding expecting mothers through their pregnancies, offering support, reassurance, expertise. This was what she did. But the moment she stepped into the clinic, she realized nothing felt quite the same.

Her first client of the day was Sophie Carter.

Sophie was in her second trimester—not too far along, just starting to show—and was coming in for a routine check-up.

More importantly, Sophie had two kids, a five-year-old and a seven-year-old.

Miranda had worked with Sophie during her last pregnancy, so the rapport was already there.

"Miranda!" Sophie greeted warmly as she walked in. "I was so excited when they told me you were back!"

Miranda smiled, setting her bag down. "It's good to be back. And how are you feeling?"

Sophie sighed dramatically, rubbing her small but noticeable baby bump. "Exhausted. Chasing after these two while growing a third is no joke."

Miranda chuckled. "I can imagine." She glanced down at the two kids clinging to Sophie's legs. "And how are my little helpers today?"

The five-year-old, Eli, grinned up at her. "Mommy said you have a baby in your tummy now, too."

Miranda blinked at the bluntness, then smiled. "That's right. I do."

The seven-year-old, Lucy, studied Miranda curiously, tilting her head. "Is your baby magic?"

Miranda's breath caught.

Sophie let out a laugh, ruffling Lucy's hair. "She's been asking that about every baby we meet lately. She's convinced Christmas magic makes babies grow faster."

Miranda forced a chuckle. "That would be convenient."

Lucy, however, didn't look convinced. She kept staring at Miranda's stomach, as if she could see something no else could.

Miranda cleared her throat. "Well, let's check in on your baby first, okay, Sophie?

Miranda measured Sophie's belly, noting her fundal height, checking her vitals—everything normal.

But as she moved through the motions, that hum inside her hadn't settled.

She felt... observed.

Not by Sophie.

By Lucy.

The little girl stood nearby, watching everything carefully, her face scrunched in concentration.

Miranda tried to ignore it, but then Lucy took a small step forward. Without saying a word, she reached out and gently placed her hand on Miranda's stomach.

Miranda froze.

Lucy's eyes widened slightly. "Your baby feels warm."

Miranda stilled completely.

Sophie, distracted by Eli, didn't seem to notice the shift in Miranda's expression.

Miranda forced a steady breath. "What do you mean, sweetheart?"

Lucy shrugged. "I don't know. He just feels... warm. Like Christmas."

Miranda's heart skipped.

Sophie finally looked up, laughing. "Lucy, what on earth does that mean?"

Lucy just grinned, rocking on her heels. "Like when it snows but you don't feel cold."

Miranda swallowed hard, willing herself to stay calm.

She finished Sophie's check-up, double checking her notes. "Everything looks great. Baby is measuring just as expected."

Sophie smiled. "That's a relief. Hopefully, this one won't come a week early like Eli."

Miranda nodded, but her mind was elsewhere.

Lucy was still watching her. Still grinning.

And as Miranda reached for her clipboard, she felt it.

That hum. That warmth.

Just for a second—a flicker of something brushing against her awareness.

A quiet, almost playful pulse of magic.

Like a child waving hello.

Miranda sucked in a breath.

Lucy giggled. "See? He knows I was talking about him."

Miranda's grip tightened slightly on the clipboard. "You're very smart, Lucy."

Lucy nodded, pleased.

And Miranda?

Miranda wasn't sure how much longer she could pretend this was normal.

<h1 style="text-align:center">37</h1>

Dr. Patel wasn't the kind of person to jump to conclusions. She dealt in facts. Science. Evidence. That was the foundation of everything she did as a physician.

But after Miranda's last appointment—after that bizarre ultrasound—Dr. Patel found herself paying closer attention.

It wasn't just the baby's elevated heart rate. That could happen for any number of benign reasons. What nagged at her was the echo. Not a visual one—a duplicate rhythm in the audio. Like two distinct beats, layered perfectly atop each other.

She had rechecked the monitor, the probe, even the software. Nothing was malfunctioning. But there was still only one baby on the screen.

A healthy one. Strong. But still... one."

And yet—two heartbeats.

At first, she told herself it was an anomaly. A blip. But the more she watched Miranda throughout the day, the harder it became to ignore.

She wasn't tired. She wasn't sluggish after a full shift back. In fact, she seemed almost...sharper. More attuned.

There were other things too. Small, subtle details only someone like Anaya would notice.

It happened during Miranda's third client of the day.

A woman named Maya Alvarez, 30 weeks pregnant with her first baby. Nervous, excited, and a little overwhelmed by all the changes happening in her body.

Miranda had always been skilled at reading her patients, at offering the right words to ease their fears. But today, Dr. Patel noticed something strange.

Maya had come in tense. She had been talking fast, shifting in her chair, rubbing at her belly anxiously.

But the moment Miranda sat beside her and started the exam, something changed.

Dr. Patel watched closely.

Miranda moved through the routine steps—measuring, checking vitals, listening. Nothing out of the ordinary.

And yet...

Maya exhaled deeply. Like she had just let go of something heavy. Her whole body had visibly relaxed, her fingers untangling from where they'd been gripping the fabric of her dress. Her pulse, which had been slightly elevated at the start of the appointment, evened out.

That's what made Anaya pause.

Miranda wasn't doing anything out of the ordinary. She wasn't speaking in a particularly soothing way. She wasn't using any calming techniques beyond her usual reassuring presence.

But Maya had settled. Almost like something unseen had nudged her into peace.

This wasn't just a woman bouncing back fast. This wasn't luck, or good nutrition, or adrenaline. This was... something else.

Anaya stared at Miranda's chart.

The baby was growing well. The blood work looked clean. And yet...

Why the echo?

She flipped to her laptop, hesitated a second, then typed:

"Fetal tachycardia with unexplained Doppler echo"

The results were vague. Most pointed to rare complications or technical error. But none of them explained the stillness she had felt while listening—that strange, synchronized rhythm that didn't feel accidental.

Anaya closed her laptop.

Something was happening. And if it wasn't coming *from* Miranda, it was coming from the *baby*.

Miranda sat at her desk, pen hovering over a chart as she stared at the numbers in front of her. She had been so sure she'd be fine. She had felt fine.

But now, at the end of her shift, the exhaustion was hitting her full force. She wasn't just tired—she was drained.

Her body ached in a way that had nothing to do with being pregnant and everything to do with the unseen weight she had been carrying all day.

And yet, no one had noticed. Because she wouldn't let them. She couldn't let them.

Miranda rolled her shoulders, blinking against the heavy fog creeping into her thoughts. *Just finish the notes. Then you can go home.*

She pressed her pen to the page, forcing herself to focus.

A soft knock at the door pulled her from her concentration.

She looked up to see Elena Morales, one of the other midwives, leaning against the frame.

"You made it through day one," Elena teased lightly, stepping inside. "How are you holding up?"

Miranda smiled automatically, masking the heaviness behind her eyes. "I'm good. Just catching up on paperwork."

Elena studied her for a moment, tilting her head slightly. "You sure? You don't even look like you had a full shift today. If I didn't know better, I'd say you're handling this return better than any of us expected."

Miranda forced a small laugh. "Well, I guess I just bounced back quicker than I thought."

Elena grinned. "Must be nice. I remember coming back after my second baby—I barely made it past lunch before I wanted to collapse."

Miranda kept her expression even. She wanted to agree. She wanted to say, "*Me too.*" But she didn't. Because she wasn't supposed to be exhausted. She had spent the whole day acting like she was fine. Like this wasn't harder than she had expected.

And yet, here she was—barely keeping her eyes open.

Elena lingered for a second longer, then shrugged. "Well, if you're ever not superhuman and need a coffee run, you know where to find me."

Miranda laughed lightly, waving her off. "I'll keep that in mind."

Elena gave a playful salute before heading back down the hall.

Miranda let out a slow, steady breath.

Superhuman. If only she felt that way.

From just outside the hallway, Anaya had been watching.

Not in an obvious way. Just enough to confirm what her instincts had already started whispering.

Miranda had moved through the day like someone on autopilot—efficient, polished, precise. Not unusual for her. But this wasn't the kind of tired you bounce back from with coffee and stubbornness. This was deeper.

The kind of tired that crept in under your skin and stayed there.

Dr. Patel frowned, shifting the file in her hands. She had expected signs of fatigue today—this was Miranda's first full day back. But she'd expected it to show sooner. Instead, Miranda hadn't slowed once. Not until now.

She saw it clearly through the half-open door: Miranda's hand resting motionless on the desk. Her shoulders sagging just enough to betray the effort it was taking to stay upright. A pause too long. A breath to shallow.

And yet... Miranda's vitals were perfect. The baby was thriving. And still, that second heartbeat—*that impossible echo*—lingered in Anaya's thoughts like a whisper she couldn't unhear.

Was this exhaustion just Miranda overworking herself?

Or was it something else entirely?

Anaya tapped her fingers absently against the folder. She knew what burnout looked like. She knew what it meant to hide it.

But this... didn't feel like burnout.

Why are you pretending, Miranda?

Miranda finally closed her last chart, her fingers stiff as she slid it into the outbox. She stood, slower than usual, her movements deliberate, as if every muscle needed instruction.

Bag slung over her shoulder, she headed for the door.

She didn't see the way Anaya watched her from the hallway.

Didn't see the thoughtful crease between her brows, or the quiet decision forming behind her eyes.

And Miranda?

Miranda had no idea she wasn't the only one keeping secrets anymore.

38

The moment Miranda stepped through the front door, the air shifted—calmer, heavier somehow.

She dropped her bag with a soft thud and let out a slow breath, one that felt like it had been waiting all day to escape.

The weight of everything pressed in—not sharply, but with that slow, sinking weariness that made even walking feel optional.

She stood there for a second, letting the hush of home wrap around her.

She turned to hang her coat and caught her reflection in the mirror beside the door—a simple, framed thing she'd walked past a hundred times.

But tonight, she paused.

The soft curve beneath her sweater was no longer something she could explain away with bloat or fatigue. It was unmistakable now.

She rested her hand over the swell, breath catching for just a moment.

"You're really in there," she whispered. Her fingers lingered as if waiting for a response.

A hundred emotions flooded her chest—wonder, fear, something deeper she didn't have a name for.

Tinsel was the first to notice.

The cat trotted over immediately, weaving between Miranda's legs, then suddenly hopping onto the armrest of the couch and staring at her with those wide, knowing eyes.

Nick wasn't far behind.

He had been in the kitchen, probably finishing up dinner, but the second he saw her, he stopped. His brows pulled together, his hands resting against the counter. He knew.

"Hey," he said gently, his voice already softer than usual. "Rough day?"

Miranda exhaled with a sound caught between laughter and disbelief. "That obvious?"

Nick gave her a look.

She didn't. Not with him. She pressed a hand to her forehead, squeezing her eyes shut for a second. "I thought I could handle it, but I'm completely wiped."

That was all it took.

Nick was already moving toward her, already reaching out as she sank onto the couch. He crouched down in front of her, resting his hands on her knees.

"Too much, too soon?"

She shook her head. "No, I—I wanted to go back. I still do. It's just... a lot."

Nick crouched in front of her again, brushing a bit of hair from her face. "Is this just from going back too fast, or... something more?"

Miranda hesitated, her hand drifting instinctively to her stomach. "It's hard to tell," she admitted. " I think it's just everything catching up to me. I'm only just into my second trimester, and I already feel like I've run a marathon."

Nick's brows lifted gently. "Wait, really? Already?"

She nodded, giving him a tired smile. "Thirteen weeks. Feels like I blinked and got here."

He let out a soft breath, his thumb rubbing gently over her knee. " I wish I could remember more... from the beginning. I feel like I missed so much."

"You didn't miss it," she said softly, reaching for his hand. "You were there. Even if you don't remember every detail, you heart was still with me the whole time."

Nick's throat bobbed slightly as he swallowed, his voice low. "Well, I'm here now. And I'm not going anywhere."

"I know," she whispered, squeezing his hand. "I just... didn't expect it to hit this hard so soon. I thought the second trimester was supposed to be the easy one."

Nick chuckled. "Yeah? Guess our kid missed the memo."

His thumb brushed lightly over her knee, the silence between them warm and understanding. He studied her face for a long moment, his gaze softening.

"You should've texted me," he murmured. "I would've come to get you."

Miranda gave a tired chuckle, sinking further into the cushions. "And let you swoop in like some overprotective hero? Imagine the rumors if the town midwife got carried out of her clinic by her husband."

Nick smirked. "Honestly? Sounds kind of iconic."

She smiled—really smiled, even through the exhaustion.

That was the thing about Nick. He never made her feel like she had to be strong all the time. He just met her where she was.

Nick exhaled, squeezing her knees lightly before standing. "Alright, lay back. I've got dinner almost done."

She blinked. "You cooked?"

He quirked a brow, teasing. "Don't sound so shocked. I am capable."

Miranda hummed. "That's debatable."

Nick rolled his eyes but grinned as he walked back into the kitchen.

Tinsel jumped onto the couch beside Miranda, settling against her side.

Miranda let out another long breath, pressing a hand lightly over her stomach.

The hum was still there. Subtle. Present

'Nick," she called.

"Yeah?" he answered from the kitchen.

She hesitated, then let her fingers trace absentmindedly over her stomach. "Something weird happened today."

Nick came back, with two plates of food in tow, his expression shifting. "Weird how?"

She told him about Lucy. The little girl who had stared at her belly. Who had called the baby "warm." Who had compared it to Christmas.

Nick didn't interrupt.

But when she finished, he sat in deep thought for a second. "Did she... say anything else?"

Miranda shook her head. "No. But, Nick, she felt something."

Nick ran a hand through his hair. "Really?"

Miranda nodded. "I know it sounds strange, but Nick... she didn't just say it like a random kid thought. She knew. She looked at me like she was certain."

Nick was quiet for a moment, his jaw tightening slightly. "What are we supposed to do with that?"

Miranda let out a slow breath. "I don't know. But I do know that this isn't just in our heads anymore. People are noticing."

Nick dragged a hand down his face. "Noticing and understanding are two different things."

Miranda watched him carefully. "You're worried."

He didn't deny it. "I just don't like not having answers." He sighed, finally meeting her gaze. "What if more people start noticing?"

Miranda hesitated, her fingers pressing lightly against her stomach. "Then we'll take it one day at a time."

Nick exhaled slowly, then nodded. One day at a time.

Miranda gave his hand a small squeeze. "Nick... we don't have to have it all figured out tonight."

Nick's lips twitched slightly, like he wanted to argue—but instead, he let out a small chuckle. "You're right. But for the record, I hate not knowing things."

Miranda smiled. "I'm aware."

Nick shook his head, rubbing her knee gently before standing. "Eat your food before you melt into the couch."

Miranda let out a tired laugh, leaning her head against the couch.. "Yes sir!"

With Miranda already in bed, Nick stood in his woodshop, the scent of sawdust and varnish grounding him as he ran his fingers over a fresh block of wood.

This was supposed to clear his head. That had been the plan—come out here, keep his hands busy, stop thinking about all the weirdness.

But the moment he picked up his carving knife, he wasn't alone. Not in a way that meant another person was there. But in a way that made his pulse stutter, his breath slow, like something unseen had settled in the space around him.

Nick frowned, rolling the block of wood between his hands. It was warm. Too warm.

Not from the heat of his palms or the temperature in the shop—something else. Something alive.

He set down the knife and pressed both hands against the surface, testing it. The warmth didn't fade.

If anything, it pulsed—faint, steady, waiting.

Nick's chest tightened. He had worked with wood all his life. He knew the difference between something reacting to touch and... whatever this was. This wasn't just wood.

It was calling to him.

Nick backed away from the workbench, scrubbing a hand over his face. This wasn't in his head. It wasn't a trick of the air, or exhaustion, or stress.

It was real. And somehow, deep in his gut, he knew what it meant.

This piece—this wood was meant for something. For someone.

For the child who hadn't even been born yet.

A slow exhale left his lips as he turned off the light, stepped out of the woodshop, and pulled the door shut behind him.

But the warmth didn't leave.

It wasn't clinging to the wood anymore—it was clinging to him.

The night air was cool against his skin, but the heat in his chest didn't fade. It wasn't overwhelming, wasn't burning, but it was there.

Nick swallowed, rolling his shoulders as he made his way up the porch steps. Maybe if he got inside, if he distracted himself, it would stop.

It didn't.

The moment he walked through the front door, the warmth shifted. Stronger now.

Pulling him.

Nick froze, his fingers flexing against his palm.

What the hell?

His gaze flicked toward the hallway, toward the soft glow of light spilling from the bedroom.

Miranda. The warmth was leading him to her.

He moved slowly, cautiously, as if expecting something to change the moment he reached the doorway.

It didn't. the warmth only deepened.

Nick pushed the door open carefully, his gaze immediately landing on Miranda.

She was curled on her side, her breathing soft and even. Tinsel was nestled near her feet, ears twitching slightly in sleep.

Everything was calm. Normal.

But the warmth inside him? Stronger than ever.

Nick hesitated, then stepped closer, his hand instinctively reaching out.

The second he touched Miranda's stomach, the world shifted.

It wasn't just warmth anymore.

It was a spark—something flickering to life deep in his mind, like embers catching flame.

A memory.

No—memories.

He saw her in the kitchen, a tray of perfectly shaped sugar cookies cooling on the counter, the scent of vanilla and sweet pea lingering in the air.

It was the middle of summer, and yet she was piping tiny snowflakes onto each one like Christmas was only a breath away.

She wore one of his flannel shirts over her pajamas, hair twisted up in a loose bun, a streak of frosting on her wrist.

When she noticed him watching, she didn't say a word—just picked up a cookie, crossed the room, and pressed it gently into his hand.

"I saved the prettiest one for you," she said with a wink.

It wasn't just the cookie that made his chest ache.

It was her.

It was always her.

The memory flooded through him, crystal clear.

But that wasn't all.

His hands worked a carving knife over smooth wood, shaping something small and delicate.

A locket.

Not just any locket—one with a hidden compartment, meant to hold a single note.

A message.

Her Christmas wish.

Her voice drifted through his mind, full of warmth and teasing af-fection.

"You always know exactly what I need before I say it."

And he had. He always had.

Until now.

Nick jerked back as if he had been burned, his breath coming faster, his heart pounding in his chest.

He staggered slightly, his fingers trembling at his side.

The warmth hadn't stopped. But now it was just a presence—it was a door.

And something inside him had just unlocked.

His gaze snapped to Miranda, still fast asleep, her brow slightly furrowed as if she had felt something too.

Tinsel was watching him.

Nick exhaled shakily, dragging a hand over his face.

He remembered. Not everything. Not enough. But pieces. More than before.

The baby wasn't just waking something in Miranda.

It was waking something in him.

Nick swallowed hard, backing away slowly before stepping out of the room.

The warmth lingered, but he knew deep down, it wasn't done with him yet.

<h1 style="text-align:center">39</h1>

The soft rustling of fabric and the quiet shuffle of feet stirred Nick from sleep. For a moment, he just listened. The faint sound of Miranda moving around the room, the zipper of a bag, the slight sigh she made as she stretched.

He blinked, adjusting to the dim morning light filtering through the curtains.

She was getting ready for work.

And for the first time in a long time, Nick had something to tell her.

Miranda had just slipped on her cardigan when she felt a presence behind her. She turned to find Nick watching her, still sitting on the edge of the bed, his hands braced against his knees. His expression was unreadable—not distant, but focused.

"Morning," she said softly, pushing a loose strand of hair behind her ear.

Nick exhaled, rubbing a hand over his face before meeting her gaze. "We need to talk."

Miranda's brow furrowed slightly, pausing in the middle of buttoning her sleeve. "About what?"

He hesitated—not because he didn't want to say it, but because he wasn't sure where to start.

Finally, he sighed. "Last night. After you went to bed."

Miranda tilted her head slightly, waiting.

Nick ran a hand through his hair. "I was in the shop. Just... clearing my head. I picked up a piece of wood, and it felt warm."

Miranda's lips parted, but she stayed quiet, letting him continue.

"Not normal warm," Nick clarified, shaking his head. "Not like from my hands or the room. It was—" He swallowed, searching for the right word. "Alive."

Miranda's breath caught.

Nick let out a short, almost incredulous chuckle. "And then I walked inside, and it didn't go away. If anything, it got stronger. Like it was... leading me somewhere."

Miranda didn't move, but he could see the recognition flicker in her expression.

"Where?" she asked quietly.

Nick's voice was steady. "To you."

Miranda's hand drifted unconsciously to her stomach. "Nick..."

He didn't let her interrupt. "I touched you, and—" His jaw tensed. "I remembered something."

Miranda inhaled softly. "What did you remember?"

Nick exhaled, his hands resting against his thighs. "More of us."

Miranda's heart pounded.

Nick lifted his gaze to hers, something raw and unshaken in his eyes. "It wasn't everything, but it was... more. I saw you in the snow, laughing. I saw you dancing. I saw—" He hesitated, his fingers twitching slightly. "A locket."

Her breath caught like a whisper trapped in her chest.

Nick watched her reaction carefully. "It was small. I carved it for you. It had a hidden compartment—some kind of message inside." His brows furrowed. "I don't remember what it said, but I remember why I made it."

Miranda's lips parted. "Nick..."

He leaned forward slightly, resting his forearms on his knees. "It's coming back, Miranda." His voice was quiet, sure. Unshaken.

Miranda swallowed hard, setting down the brush she had been holding. "This baby... it's waking something in you, isn't it?"

Nick nodded. "Yeah. I think it is."

A heavy silence settled between them—not tense, not fearful. Just... full.

Miranda stepped closer, reaching out to run her fingers lightly through his hair. He closed his eyes briefly at the touch, leaning into her warmth.

When he opened them again, there was no doubt left. No brushing it off. No calling it strange. No trying to rationalize it. He had felt it. He had seen it.

And now? Now, he believed it.

Miranda's thumb brushed against his cheek. "Are you okay?"

Nick huffed a quiet laugh, shaking his head. "Not even a little."

She smiled, pressing a soft kiss to his forehead. "We'll figure it out. Together."

Nick sighed, his shoulders easing. His hand found its way to her stomach again, resting lightly.

"I don't know how we will," he said quietly. "But if it's with you... I believe we can."

For the first time since the accident, Nick didn't feel like he was grasping at shadows.

For the first time, he felt like he was coming home.

40

Miranda barely had time to sit down between appointments when Sarah knocked on her office door.

"Miranda, we've got two laboring moms coming in—Emma Gradson and Claire Dawson. Both are asking for you."

Miranda straightened. "What's their status?"

Sarah checked her notes. "Emma just arrived, early labor progressing slow, but Claire's contractions are strong. Dr. Langford thinks she's close."

Miranda nodded, already switching gears. Two labors at once. Not uncommon, but never easy.

"Alright, I'll check on Claire first, then see where Emma is."

Sarah nodded, already moving. Miranda grabbed her chest, rolled her shoulders, and followed.

Claire Dawson had been laboring at home as long as she could stand it, arriving at the clinic already deep into labor.

Miranda entered to find Claire gripping the hospital bed rails, her face tense with concentration. Her husband, Mark, stood beside her, whispering encouragement as another contraction rolled through.

Miranda moved quickly, checking the monitors and gently examining her.

Nine centimeters. Almost there.

She squeezed Claire's hand. "You're doing incredible. Not much longer now."

Claire gave a shaky nod, sucking in a deep breath as the contraction passed. "I just—" she exhaled. "I just want him here."

Miranda smiled. "He'll be here soon."

She turned to Sarah. "Let's get the delivery team prepped. She's almost ready."

Claire leaned back, eyes closed. "Please don't leave yet."

Miranda hesitated. She needed to check on Emma, but Claire's urgency tugged at something deep inside her.

Still, she had to move. "I'll be right back, I promise."

Claire nodded, clutching her husband's hand.

Across the hall, Emma Gradson's experience was very different.

She sat propped against pillows, looking exhausted but nowhere near delivery.

Her contractions were still too far apart.

Miranda entered with a soft smile. "Hey, Emma. How are you feeling?"

Emma groaned, rubbing her lower back. "Like this baby is never coming."

Miranda chuckled, checking her chart. "You're making progress, just slowly."

Emma sighed dramatically. "So, I'm in for the long haul?"

Miranda nodded sympathetically. "Looks like it. But you're doing great. Have you eaten or had anything to drink?"

Emma shook her head, and Miranda frowned. "Okay, let's fix that. You need to keep your energy up."

Emma made a face. "I don't feel like eating."

Miranda's lips curved with teasing familiarity. "You will later. Let's at least try something light."

Emma sighed, defeated. "Fine."

Miranda gave her a reassuring squeeze on the arm. "One way or another, this baby is coming. I promise."

For the next two hours, Miranda bounced between both rooms.

Claire was progressing fast. Every time Miranda checked in, she was closer, her body working hard to bring her baby into the world.

Emma, on the other hand, was stuck in the slow crawl of early labor. Her contractions weren't picking up the way they should.

Miranda knew she had to balance the two—giving Emma time and encouragement while staying close for Claire.

She'd done this before. But today, something felt different.

Not physically. Not yet.

But there was a hum beneath her skin, something deep and unshakable, like her body knew she was guiding two babies into the world today.

Miranda didn't have time to dwell on it.

Because Claire was ready.

The final stage came fast.

Claire, exhausted but determined, pushed through the last contractions.

Mark held her hand, whispering encouragement, his voice thick with emotion.

Miranda stayed steady, guiding her through each breath, each push.

And then—

A final cry. A baby's first breath.

Claire collapsed back against the pillows, laughing and crying all at once as her newborn son was placed on her chest.

Mark choked out a breathless laugh, brushing his wife's hair back. "He's here."

Miranda smiled, stepping back slightly to let them have their moment. This. This was why she did this. But she wasn't done.

Sarah caught her eye. "Emma's contractions are finally picking up."

Miranda nodded, taking a steadying breath.

She still had another baby to bring into the world. And for some reason, her body knew it.

Emma was finally in active labor and Miranda was starting to feel it.

Her legs felt heavier, her breathing wasn't labored but she felt a weight in her chest, and her hands just felt... slower.

Nothing noticeable to anyone else. Except for Dr. Patel.

She hadn't been looking for signs of exhaustion—not at first.

But the longer she watched, the harder it was to ignore.

Miranda wasn't slowing down, not exactly, but there was a shift—a subtle drag in her movements, a quiet weight behind her breath.

Miranda wasn't okay.

Dr. Patel narrowed her eyes, making a mental note.

She wasn't about to confront Miranda now. Not while she was in the middle of guiding another birth.

But after?

After, she'd have questions.

Unlike Claire's quick and intense labor, Emma's had been a slow burn.

Her contractions were strong but spaced apart. The hours had stretched on, exhaustion creeping into her expression.

Miranda knew this kind of labor well.

The kind that drained a mother before the real work even began.

Emma clenched the bedsheets as another contraction rolled through. "I don't— I don't think I can do this anymore."

Her husband, seated at her side, squeezed her hand. "You're doing amazing, Em."

Miranda knelt beside the bed, her voice calm but firm. "Your body is working exactly how it's supposed to. You're progressing, I promise."

Emma shook her head, tears welling. "It's just—its taking so long."

Miranda nodded, her heart aching for her. She had seen this countless times before. The exhaustion. The doubt.

"You're tired, I know," Miranda said gently. "But you are not stuck. Your body is moving forward, and I need you to trust that, even when it feels impossible."

Emma let out a shaky breath, searching Miranda's eyes.

Miranda held her gaze, her voice steadier now—anchored by something deeper. "You were created for this. God made your body to do this very thing. I know it feels endless right now, but your baby is not far."

She reached up and gently brushed a tear from Emma's cheek. "All of this? It's not wasted. Every ache, every hour—it's building toward something holy. The baby is your reward, and you are almost there."

Emma swallowed hard, then nodded.

She wasn't ready yet. But she would be and Miranda would be there every step of the way.

Lord, give her strength. Carry her when she feels she can't go on. You made her for this—help her believe it. Amen.

Time stretched.

Emma breathed through each contraction, her body slowly but surely bringing her baby closer.

Miranda didn't leave her side. She should have taken a break. She should have sat down, let another midwife step in for a while. But she couldn't, because Emma needed her. And Miranda had promised.

Then—finally.

Emma let out a gasping breath as a contraction hit harder than the ones before.

Her eyes widened in panic. "I feel—I feel pressure."

Miranda straightened. "Alright. Let's check."

She moved quickly, examining her, a rush of relief settling in.

"You're ready. Baby is right there."

Emma sobbed out a half-laugh. "Oh, thank God."

Her husband pressed a shaky kiss to her forehead. "You did it, babe."

Miranda smiled. "Not yet, but almost."

The nurses prepped the room, the warmth of anticipation replacing the weight of exhaustion.

Emma clenched her husband's hand. "Okay. Okay. Let's do this."

"Let's do this."

Emma fought for every push.

She was exhausted, her body working hard, but she never stopped.

The room filled with anticipation.

Then—

A final push and baby was here.

Emma was overjoyed as her daughter was placed on her chest.

Miranda, breathless despite herself, let out a quiet exhale.

The slowest labor of the day, but finally, the baby was here.

Emma sobbed as she cradled her daughter against her chest, pressing a trembling kiss to her forehead.

Her husband let out a shaky laugh, eyes wet. "She's perfect."

Miranda felt it too. The joy. The relief. The end of a long, long day.

She placed a hand on Emma's shoulder, squeezing gently. "You did it Momma!"

Emma let out a watery chuckle. "We did it Miranda."

41

Miranda lay curled on the small couch in her office, one arm draped over her eyes as she tried to will her body to move. It wasn't working. The exhaustion had settled deep into her bones, making the quiet hum of the room feel like a lullaby she couldn't escape.

The door creaked open.

"And here I thought I was the dramatic one," came Dr. Patel's voice, dry as ever. "What, no fainting chaise? No pearl clutching?"

Miranda groaned softly, not lifting her arm. "Give me five minutes and a hot compress, and I'll try again."

Anaya stepped inside, shutting the door behind her. "Long day, huh?"

"Understatement of the year," Miranda mumbled.

She finally peeled her arm away and looked up at her friend. "I'm not dying. Just melting."

Anaya leaned against the doorframe, her grin full of mischief. "Do I need to start bringing electrolytes and a fan to work? Maybe a tiny violin?"

"You already bring the judgment. Might as well accessorize," Miranda shot back with a faint smile.

"Touche." Anaya crossed the room and perched on the arm of the couch. "I'm not going to give you a speech about resting. I figured you'd just ignore it."

Miranda's smile faded slightly. "I know. I'm trying. It's just... a lot."

Anaya studied her for a moment, the teasing leaving her eyes. "Anything feel different today? Besides the obvious?"

Miranda hesitated. "You mean besides the crushing fatigue and the sudden urge to cry over a granola bar?"

Anaya chuckled. "Exactly that."

There was a beat of silence before Miranda sat up a little straighter, one hand resting instinctively on her belly. "Something happened yesterday. A little girl—I was checking on her mom—and she touched my stomach. Said it felt warm. Almost like Christmas."

Anaya's eyebrows lifted slightly.

"And I know kids say strange things all the time," Miranda added quickly, "but she wasn't guessing. She knew. She felt something."

Anaya leaned in, her voice low. "And you think there's truth to it."

Miranda nodded. "I do. And honestly... It scared me a little. Not in a bad way. Just... It reminded me that this isn't normal. None of this is."

Anaya didn't speak. Her eyes searched Miranda's face, trying to piece together the threads of something she didn't dare to name.

"There's more I haven't told you," Miranda said softly. She looked down, brushing her fingers lightly across her belly. "I wasn't sure I ever would. But I think you already know, at least part of it. You've seen it."

Anaya waited.

Miranda took a breath, then finally met her gaze. "This baby... isn't just special. He's something special... and so am I."

She hesitated, then continued, her voice quieter. "Before the pregnancy, it was easier to hide. I could brush things off, keep my distance, pretend the strange moments were just coincidence. But now... the magic is stronger. The baby's amplifying it. I can't control when it shows up anymore. And people are starting to notice."

She looked down. "You're my closest friend, Anaya. And you're the only one I trust enough to tell. Because I need someone who doesn't just see what's happening, but believes it too. I've been holding this secret for over a hundred years, and now it's getting harder to carry alone."

The words hovered between them, delicate and dangerous.

"It's Nick," Miranda said softly. "He's Santa Claus. The real one"

She paused only for a breath.

"And I'm Mrs. Claus."

Anaya blinked. "I'm sorry—what?"

"I know how it sounds," Miranda said gently, holding her gaze. "But it's true. Nick is Santa. I've been by his side since the 1920's. I don't age. I don't get sick—at least, I didn't."

She paused, her hand resting over her belly.

"Since Nick's accident, our magic has been weaker. And now, being pregnant for the first time… everything feels different. Harder."

Her voice softened. "And this baby—he's already showing signs of something I don't fully understand. It's like he knows things. Like he's guiding me, even now."

Anaya sat back, stunned. "You're telling me that *you're* Mrs. Claus. As in… the actual Mrs. Claus."

Miranda nodded. "I know it sounds insane."

"That's putting it gently." She rubbed a hand over her face. "This is a stress response. Or a hallucination. Or you've read one too many holiday books and your brain finally snapped."

"I'm telling the truth Anaya."

"And you're serious," Anaya muttered, staring at her like she was a puzzle that had finally scrambled itself too far. "You actually believe this."

"I've lived it."

Another long silence. Anaya crossed her arms tightly and sat down. Her eyes scanned Miranda's face again, searching for cracks.

"You don't age," she said slowly. "You always seem to know exactly what someone needs before they say it. And Tinsel—your cat is *definitely* not normal."

Miranda gave a faint smile. "She's very selective."

Anaya exhaled, still trying to wrap her head around what she's hearing. "This isn't happening. Santa Claus isn't real."

Miranda's tone didn't change. "And yet here I am. Still twenty-nine years old, after over a century. Married to a man who delivers joy to the world every year. And somehow, I've managed to keep it quiet... until now."

Anaya stared at her like she was waiting for the punchline. When none came, she sank further into her chair. "This is either the weirdest fever dream I've ever had," she muttered, "or I need to get my brain scanned."

"I get it," Miranda said. "I'd be reacting the same way."

"You're not lying," Anaya said at last, like the words surprised even her. "Are you?"

"No."

Anaya was quiet for a long moment. Then she let out a slow, almost stunned breath and shook her head with a half-laugh—one without humor.

"Well... okay," she said finally. "I believe you. I don't know how, or why, but—I do."

Miranda let her shoulders relax, just slightly.

"But you have to understand," Anaya added quickly, her voice regaining its usual edge, "you've just upended the laws of biology, time, and physics in under five minutes. So, yeah, I've got questions."

Miranda smiled softly. "Ask away."

Anaya narrowed her eyes. "First off—this baby. You keep calling it a he. But we haven't done the anatomy scan yet. How do you know?"

Miranda glanced down at her belly, her hand still resting there with gentle reverence. "I just do," she said. "It's like he's been with me from the start. Not just growing inside me—but watching, knowing, guiding me. And Nick. He moved when I'm uncertain.

Calms when I'm afraid. It's more than intuition—it's like... he's aware."

Anaya blinked. "So we're adding fetal sentience to the list now."

Miranda laughed softly. "Add whatever you want. But he's real. And he's special. I feel it in every part of me."

Anaya didn't speak for a few seconds. Then she rubbed her hands over her face again. "Okay. Santa's real. You're his wife. Your unborn child is possibly a magical empath. I should've brought wine."

Mirand reached for her hand. "I know it's a lot. But thank you... for believing me."

Anaya gave her a look—half overwhelmed, half fiercely loyal. "Don't thank me yet. I'm still deciding if this makes you a miracle... or my most complicated case to date."

She leaned back in her chair with a groan. "Honestly, I might just cancel science altogether. What's the point? Apparently, magic babies are out here rewriting biology and no one thought to tell me."

Miranda smiled, the weight on her chest finally easing a little.

Anaya pointed at her, narrowing her eyes. "But you? You need to go home. Rest. Maybe eat something enchanted. Whatever it is you do."

"I don't have enchanted snacks," Miranda said with a tired laugh.

"Well, you should," Anaya muttered. "And I better not find out your gingerbread men wink at people, or I'm out."

Miranda laughed again, then hesitated as she stood, her hand resting gently over her stomach.

Her voice softened. "Anaya... no one else can know. Not yet. Just you."

Anaya's teasing expression faded into something more serious. She nodded once. "You've got my word."

Miranda met her gaze for a long moment, then finally exhaled.

"Okay," she whispered. "Then I'll go home."

Anaya stood with her, giving her arm a gentle squeeze. "Good. And for the record? You're the weirdest miracle I've met."

The moment Miranda stepped through the front door, barely had time to drop her bag before Tinsel was there.

The cat trotted toward her from the living room, tail flicking high, ears perked. But something was different. Tinsel didn't just greet her. She stared.

Miranda sighed as she kicked off her shoes. "Hey, Tinsel."

Tinsel didn't meow in greeting like she usually did. Instead, she sat at Miranda's feet, looking up at her. She looked more concerned than anything.

Miranda let out a tired chuckle. "Don't look at me like that. I had a long day, okay?"

She bent down to scratch behind Tinsel's ears, but the cat didn't lean into it. She bumped her head into Miranda's stomach instead.

The cat sat back again, blinking up at her. Waiting.

Miranda exhaled slowly, pressing a hand to her belly. "Yeah," she murmured. "I know."

"Hey, you're home—" Nick's voice cut off mid-sentence.

She looked up just as he stepped into the entryway, his expression shifting the moment he saw her. The exhaustion must have been written all over her face, because his whole demeanor changed in an instant.

The casual ease disappeared. Replaced by concern. He took one step closer, brows drawing together. "Miranda!"

She sighed, already knowing what was coming. "Nick, I'm fine."

His gaze flicked from her face to her posture. The slight slump in her shoulders and the way she was pressing a hand against the doorframe, as if she needed the support.

He shook his head. "No. You're not."

Miranda huffed out a breath, tired but amused. "You act like I just crawled through the door."

Nick gave her a look, "You might as well have."

Before she could protest, he was already moving.

Closing the distance, his hands landed on her waist. He wasn't rough—just steady. Solid.

After a moment, Miranda sighed, letting her weight settle against him.

"Okay," she muttered. "Maybe I overdid it."

Nick huffed out something that was half a laugh, half a relieved exhale.

"Yeah," he murmured, pressing a quick kiss to her forehead. "Maybe."

Miranda let her eyes drift shut for a second before pulling back.

Nick didn't let her go. "Come on," he said softly. "Couch. Now."

She didn't argue and sank onto the cushions, exhaling slowly as the weight of the day settled in.

And then—Tinsel jumped up beside her. Not lazily but with a purpose. She landed near Miranda's hip, then circled once before settling in—pressing firmly against her side. As if staking her claim and standing guard at the same time.

"Today was... a lot"

Nick settled beside her, resting his arm along the back of the couch. "Tell me about it."

She sighed, tilting her head slightly to look at him. "You really want to hear about a full day of contractions and labors?"

Nick gave her a sideways grin. "I listen to you talk about birth stuff all the time. Might as well keep the streak going."

Miranda chuckled, the sound light despite her being so tired. "Alright. Fair enough." She shifted slightly, tucking her legs beneath her. "I had two moms in labor at the same time today."

Nick's brows lifted. "Two? That explains why you look like you haven't sat down in hours."

"I laid down for maybe ten minutes," she muttered. "Doesn't feel like it helped."

Nick's lips twitched, "Go on."

A soft breath left her as she remembered. "One of them went fast. She barely made it through the door before she was ready to push. The other? She had a long, slow labor. She was exhausted before she even got to delivery.

Nick studied her. "And you didn't stop moving between the two, did you?"

Miranda rubbed her temple. "I couldn't. They both needed me."

Nick hummed, watching her closely. "And when did you need you?

Miranda hesitated.

Nick arched a brow, "Exactly."

She shook her head, amused despite herself. "You sound like Anaya."

Nick grinned. "Good. She's a smart woman."

Miranda laughed, but Nick didn't miss the way her body sagged slightly against the cushions. She was done.

He brushed his knuckles against her knee, his voice quieter now. "Was it a good day, at least?"

Miranda thought about that.

Despite the exhaustion.

Despite the non-stop hours, the juggling, the feeling like she barely had time to breathe.

She thought about Claire's first sob of relief when she held her baby.

About Emma's stunned laughter when she realized she had finally done it.

And about the quiet, sacred moment of witnessing life begin again.

She let out a slow breath.

"Yeah," she murmured. "It was a good day."

Nick smiled. "Then it was worth it."

Miranda nodded, eyes drooping slightly.

Nick shifted closer, brushing a hand over her arm. "Come on. Let's get you to bed."

Miranda hummed. "I might sleep here."

Nick snorted. "Not happening."

She sighed, but didn't argue when he helped her up.

Tinsel followed them down the hall, tail flicking as if making sure Miranda actually went to bed.

Nick caught it, smirking slightly.

"I think she likes me a little more today," He teased.

Miranda chuckled sleepily. "She just wants to make sure you don't let me fall asleep standing up."

Nick didn't deny it. Instead, he guided her into the bedroom, tucking her under the blankets before passing a soft kiss to her forehead.

"Sleep," he murmured.

Miranda sighed, already drifting.

And for the first time all day, she finally let herself rest.

<h1 style="text-align:center">42</h1>

Miranda didn't need to be told to stay home. For once, her body made the call before her mind had the chance to argue.

She woke to the sound of birds outside the window and the faint creak of floorboards down the hall—Nick, probably heading toward the kitchen. Morning light filtered through the curtains, soft and golden, and the weight of the covers felt heavier than usual.

Not unpleasant. Just...final.

She let herself breathe in it for a moment. No rush. No pressure. Just stillness.

By the time Nick returned with a mug of tea in one hand and a plate in the other, she was sitting up against the pillows, hair tousled and cheeks still flushed from sleep.

"Good," he said, setting the tea down on the nightstand. "You're awake. I made you something."

Miranda looked at the toast and sliced pear on the plate with mild suspicion. "This feels suspiciously like bribery."

Nick grinned. "No. This is domestic manipulation. Very different."

She rolled her eyes, but took the tea. "You're lucky I'm too tired to argue."

He didn't press her about work. Didn't mention the clinic or emails or to-do lists. He just sat beside her and waited while she ate slowly, content to be near.

They didn't speak much. But it wasn't awkward. Just quiet. Gentle.

Eventually, Miranda set the empty plate aside and leaned her head on his shoulder.

"I think I'll stay home today," she said, barely above a whisper.

Nick smiled without looking at her. "I know."

It was closer to ten when the knock came.

Nick was the one who answered the door, but Mirand already knew who it was.

She was curled up on the couch, wrapped in a throw blanket, half-watching the fire in the fireplace when Anaya stepped inside.

"You look like someone who finally gave in," Anaya said by way of greeting, slipping off her coat.

Miranda didn't sit up. "I surrendered gracefully. No glares, no clipboard in hand. Be proud."

"I am proud," Anaya said, settling into the armchair like she belonged there. "And mildly suspicious."

Nick handed her a mug of coffee, then excused himself to the back porch, sensing they needed space.

For a few minutes, neither of them spoke. Anaya sipped her coffee. Miranda stared at the fire. The silence felt different than usual—closer.

Anaya was the one who broke it. "I haven't stopped thinking about what you told me."

Miranda didn't respond right away. She just stared into the fire, the silence between them deepening.

"It's not every day someone casually drops that they're Mrs. Claus."

Miranda gave a soft, humorless laugh. "I figured it might take a minute to sink in."

Anaya leaned forward, elbows on her knees, coffee cradled in both hands. "I'm still not sure whether I want to run labs or hug you."

"Both would be on brand."

"But seriously," Anaya said, voice quieter now. "How are you holding up? After carrying that secret for so long?"

Miranda's hand drifted over her belly. "It was easier before the baby. Before Nick's accident. Now... it feels heavier. Louder. Like something shifting, and I don't know what it means yet."

Anaya just nodded, no longer trying to make sense of it through logic. Just listening.

They sat for a while, the silence no longer awkward but full of unspoken questions.

Anaya glanced around the living room like she was seeing it differently now. "You know, looking back... it makes sense. Sort of."

Miranda raised a brow. "Sort of?"

"You've always had that thing about you. The weird calm. The way you make people feel safe just by being in the room."

Miranda smiled faintly. "It's just who I am."

"No," Anaya said, shaking her head. "It's more than that. I used to think you were just really good at reading people. But now? I'm starting to wonder if the baby didn't get it from you."

Miranda looked down, brushing her fingers gently over her stomach. "He's been quiet today. Watching. Listening."

Anaya tilted her head. "You really believe he's aware."

"I don't just believe it," Miranda said softly. "I know."

There was a pause, something unspoken hanging in the air. Then Miranda glanced up at her, a little smile playing at her lips.

"Come here."

Anaya blinked. "What?"

"Just... come here."

She hesitated, but curiosity won out. Anaya crossed the room slowly and knelt beside the couch. Miranda gently took her hand and guided it to rest over the curve of her belly.

They sat like that for a beat, the quiet stretching long.

And then Anaya stilled.

It was subtle—barely there—but something warm pulsed beneath her hand. Not movement. Not a kick. Just... presence. Like a quiet shimmer in the air, blooming from deep within Miranda and wrapping around them both.

Anaya gasped in awe.

"What was that?" she whispered, eyes wide.

Miranda didn't move. "He's saying hello."

Anaya looked at her, stunned. "That wasn't in my head."

"No."

"It felt like..." She trailed off, searching for the right words. "Like standing in sunlight. But from the inside."

Miranda smiled. "That's him."

Anaya sat back slowly, her hand still hovering just above Miranda's belly, as if afraid to break the moment.

"Okay," she said at last, voice barely above a breath. "I believe you. I *really* believe you."

Before Miranda could respond, the back door creaked open and footsteps crossed the wood floor.

Nick stepped into the room, eyes immediately going to the two of them. He took in the stillness, the look on Anaya's face, the warmth in Miranda's expression.

He paused, coffee mug in hand. "...Did I miss something?"

Anaya slowly turned her head toward him, dazed. "Your child just radiated light into my bones."

Nick blinked. "I'm sorry—what?"

Miranda laughed softly, reaching for his hand. "It's fine. He's just... making friends."

Nick looked between the two of them, clearly confused but trusting. "Is this the kind of thing I'm supposed to pretend makes sense?"

"Yes," Miranda and Anaya said in unison.

Nick nodded slowly, then leaned down to press a kiss to Miranda's temple. "Noted."

He straightened and looked at Anaya. "You good?"

She just shook her head. "Absolutely not. But I'll figure it out later."

Nick looked between the two women again, still visibly thrown but trying to keep up. "Should I be concerned?"

Anaya stood, brushing her hands on her jeans like she needed to ground herself. "No. I mean—yes. I mean..." She exhaled. "You have a very opinionated fetus. That's all I'm going to say."

Miranda chuckled. "Thank you for coming."

Anaya pointed at her on her way to the door. "No working today. No emails. No 'just checking in' texts to Lydia. If I even smell a calendar reminder, I'm turning this place into a no-wifi zone."

"Threat received," Miranda said, grinning.

Anaya gave Nick a lingering glance. "Take care of her."

"Always," he said, no hesitation.

Anaya opened the door, then looked back one last time. "And next time? Warn me before your baby beams Christmas joy through my sternum."

She disappeared with the swirl of the wind, and the door clicked shut behind her.

For a moment, the house was quiet again.

Nick stepped closer, his eyes searching Miranda's face. "You okay?"

She nodded. "Yeah. I think I am."

He sat beside her on the couch, resting a hand on her knee. "So... are we gonna talk about what just happened, or should I just accept that our unborn child is glowing like a holiday nightlight now?"

Miranda leaned into him, resting her head on his shoulder. "I'll explain everything. I promise. Just... not yet."

Nick's arm wrapped around her, steady and sure. "Take your time."

They sat there for a while, tangled in quiet.

And for the first time in days, Miranda didn't feel like she was un-
raveling.

She felt held.

Known.

Home.

<h1 style="text-align:center">43</h1>

Miranda shifted on the couch for what felt like the hundredth time, the blanket tangled around her legs and Tinsel pressed firmly against her side like a tiny, judgmental bodyguard.

"I'm just stretching," she muttered aloud, as if that would convince the cat she wasn't trying to sneak off and alphabetize the prenatal supplement shelf.

Tinsel's eyes narrowed. She didn't budge.

Miranda sighed and leaned her head back against the cushion. The house was quiet. The kind of quiet she usually loved. But today it pressed against her in a strange way. Like the stillness wasn't offering peace, but asking her to sit with everything she'd just admitted.

Anaya had been gentle that morning— unusually so—but her words hadn't lost their edge.

"No work. No emails. No 'just check in' texts to Lydia."

There had been no sarcasm. No raised brow. Just sincerity. Steady and unwavering. The kind that felt like a warm hand on your back when the world was too loud.

And that, somehow, made Miranda feel even more raw.

Because Anaya knew now.

And she'd stayed.

She hadn't laughed or asked for proof. She hadn't pulled out a stethoscope or demanded a blood panel. She'd just believed.

And then—when the baby pulsed his magic through Miranda's belly and into Anaya's hand—she didn't run. She didn't rationalize.

She felt it.

Miranda looked down at her stomach, her hand resting gently over the soft curve. That warmth was still there, steady and quiet. Not movement. Not a flutter. Just presence.

Tinsel let out a low purr beside her, as if she could sense it too.

For the first time since speaking the truth aloud, Miranda allowed herself to settle into it. To own it.

Mrs. Claus.

It wasn't just a role. It wasn't some mantle she carried behind the scenes. It was *her*. It always had been.

But now... someone else knew. Someone who mattered.

Anaya looked at her like she was more than a story. Like she was real.

And Miranda?

She didn't feel so alone anymore.

She closed her eyes. Not to sleep—just to breathe.

The silence around didn't feel like it was closing in anymore.

It felt like it was holding her.

Nick tucked his wallet into his back pocket as he stepped into the soft bustle of the Fir Hollow Saturday Market. Booths lined the narrow road beside the library, each one filled with the sights and smells of early spring—lavender soaps, honey jars, handmade jewelry, fresh bread still warm in its wrapping.

He didn't tell Miranda why he was really going out. Just that he needed to "grab a few things." She hadn't questioned it. Maybe too tired to care, maybe trusting him to come back with something she didn't know she needed.

But something had been off that morning.

Not with Miranda—at least, not in the way she might have thought. She looked exhausted, sure, but there was something else under the surface. A quiet shift between her and Anaya. Something unspoken.

And it stuck with him.

Nick passed a booth with polished wood carvings and paused without meaning to. One of the ornaments—round and etched with tiny reindeer—caught his eye. His hand moved toward it instinctively, and for a moment, his fingers tingled. Familiar. Like a shape he'd held a thousand times before but couldn't place.

The vendor smiled at him. "Beautiful craftsmanship, huh?"

Nick nodded slowly, his gaze lingering.

"Handmade," the vendor added. "Local wood. Most people buy them around Christmas, but they look nice all year."

Nick opened his mouth to respond, but no words came.

A gust of wind passed through the market. The scent of cinnamon, fir, and something almost like snow brushed over him, even though the sky was clear.

He shook his head, clearing the strange fog, and smiled politely before moving on. It wasn't until he caught the sound of a familiar voice that he stopped in his tracks.

"Mom, do we have to get the round bread again? I want the twisty one this time!"

Nick approached slowly, unsure if Leon would remember him.

He didn't have to wonder long.

Leon's face lit up the moment he looked up. "Hey! It's Mr. Nick!"

Nick smiled. "Hey, kiddo."

Leon jumped to his feet. "Look! No cast anymore!" He held out his arm proudly, flexing it as if showing off a superhero badge. "The doctor said my bones are all good now."

Nick chuckled. "That's great news. You healing fast must mean you've been eating your veggies."

Leon wrinkled his nose. "Ugh. Don't remind me."

Nick glanced up just as Evelyn turned toward them, a paper bag of bread tucked under her arm. She spotted Nick and gave a warm but surprised smile as she walked over.

Evelyn looked up as Nick approached, surprise flickering across her face. "Well, this is a nice surprise," she said with a smile.

"Not interrupting anything, I hope?" Nick asked.

"Just getting some fresh air and browsing," she replied. "Everything alright?"

Nick nodded. "Yeah, just... out looking for something. For Miranda."

Evelyn tilted her head. "Oh? Special occasion?"

Nick gave a small smile. "Not exactly. She's pregnant."

Evelyn's eyes lit up. "Really? That's wonderful!"

"She hasn't told many people yet," he added. "We've been keeping it quiet for a while."

"How's she doing?" Evelyn said warmly.

"She's tired," Nick said honestly. "Today she finally decided to slow down and rest. I just wanted to get her something... I don't know. A little reminder that I see her. That I'm proud of her."

Evelyn's expression softened instantly. "That's beautiful, Nick. She's lucky to have you."

Nick shook his head. "I'm the lucky one."

Leon piped up again, "You should get her one of those little crystal things. My grandma says they help with energy and feelings."

Nick arched a brow. "Do they?"

Leon shrugged. "She says a blue one helps your brain feel less like scrambled eggs. That could help you too."

Evelyn gave an apologetic glance, but Nick just laughed. "Actually... that might be the best suggestion I've heard all day."

He paused, thoughtful. "Do you mind if I steal him for a minute?"

Evelyn raised a brow. "To do what?"

Nick lifted a brow, teasing. "Crystal shopping."

Twenty minutes later, Nick walked back toward his truck with a small paper bag in hand. Inside was a tiny polished stone, a pale bluish-green shimmer to it that the vendor had called "Amazonite."

The card tucked beside it said:

"Peace, balance, and clarity."

"A reminder to rest, breathe, and believe."

Leon had picked it out, after touching nearly every stone on the table and declaring this one "felt like soft music."

Nick wasn't sure if he believed in crystals or their energy.

But he believed in gestures.

And he believed in Miranda.

As Nick left the market, something made him glance over his shoulder. A man stood near the far edge of the stalls, just past the maple trees. Hands in his coat pockets. Too still. Watching. But when Nick turned to look again. The man was gone.

When he returned home, the cottage was quiet.

Miranda was fast asleep beneath the red and white blanket on the couch, her breathing deep and steady. Tinsel lay sprawled across her belly like a sentry, one eye half open as Nick slipped quietly through the room.

He set the bag on the coffee table, beside the cold mug of tea Miranda had likely forgotten she made.

Then he sat across from her, resting his elbows on his knees, and just watched her sleep for a while.

He didn't know what was coming next.

But in that moment, with the faint sound of the breeze brushing against the windows, and the snowflake charm still warm in his pocket...

He knew he wasn't going anywhere.

Miranda stirred an hour later, blinking sluggishly against the afternoon light. She stretched, wincing slightly at the stiffness in her joints.

Nick, still in the chair across from her, immediately sat forward.

Miranda groaned, rubbing her eyes. "Tell me I didn't sleep all day."

Nick nudged her gently, amusement playing at his mouth. "Just an hour. But if you tried, I bet you could make it 'til morning."

She rolled her eyes, sitting up slowly. Tinsel begrudgingly moved but didn't go far.

Nick hesitated for half a second before speaking. "I've been thinking," he said carefully.

Miranda stilled, instantly catching the shift in his tone. She turned to him, brows furrowing slightly. "About what?"

Nick exhaled, running a hand through his hair. "The other day. What happened in the shop. What happened when I touched your stomach."

Miranda blinked, still shaking off sleep. But now, she was fully alert.

Nick leaned forward, resting his forearms on his knees.

"I can't shake it, Miranda. The warmth, the memories coming back. It wasn't just in my head."

Miranda studied him carefully. He wasn't hesitant, wasn't brushing it off anymore.

He was serious. And more than that—he was ready to talk about it.

Miranda swallowed, sitting up fully now. "Okay. Let's talk about it," she said softly. "So... what does this mean?"

Nick's fingers twitched against his knee. "I don't know."

Miranda tilted her head, searching his face. "You remembered something. More than just flashes—actual memories. That's... not small, Nick."

Nick exhaled slowly. "I know."

She watched him carefully. "So... do you think it's all coming back?"

Nick ran a hand through his hair. "I don't know if it's that simple." He let out a humorless chuckle. "It's not like I woke up this morning remembering everything. But... something's shifting. It's happening."

Miranda nodded slowly. "And it's not just random memories. They're all connected to us."

Nick's jaw tightened slightly, but he didn't deny it.

Miranda hesitated, then asked the real question that had been sitting in her chest since that night.

"Do you feel like... you're starting to remember who you really are?"

His lungs stalled for a second. No reply came.

Miranda watched the conflict play across his face—the struggle between what he knew, what he felt, and what he couldn't explain yet.

Finally, he sighed, rubbing his temples.

"I don't know," he admitted. "But I think... I think I'm starting to."

Miranda's heart clenched.

Because that was the first real step.

He might not have all the answers yet, but for the first time, he was acknowledging that there was more to him than what he currently remembered.

She reached for his hand, squeezing gently. "Then that's enough for now."

Nick exhaled, looking down at their hands, then back at her. "Yeah," he murmured. And for the first time since the accident, he almost believed it.

Miranda glanced over at the coffee table, her gaze landing on the small paper bag she hadn't noticed before. "What's this?"

Nick rubbed the back of his neck. "Something I found at the market. Leon helped me pick it out."

She opened the bag slowly, curious. Inside, nestled in tissue paper, was a smooth bluish-green stone. The light caught on its surface, shimmering like water.

A tiny card slipped out with it:

"Peace, balance, and clarity."

"A reminder to rest, breathe, and believe."

Miranda stared at it, emotions rising too quickly to name. "It's beautiful," she said quietly.

Nick shrugged, a little sheepish. "Didn't know if you were a crystal person."

"I don't know if I am either," she said, holding the stone to her palm. "But this? This feels exactly right."

She looked up at him—and in that moment, something clicked.

A flicker.

A memory, soft and faded at the edges.

They were younger. A different living room, dust motes dancing in the light of a window frosted with snow. Miranda sat cross-legged on the floor, unwrapping a small parcel—a snow globe, hand-painted, with two deer nestled beneath a tree. She looked up at him with that same look. That same smile. Like he had just handed her the world.

The scent of cinnamon lingered in the air. Tinsel had been curled up under the tree, blinking lazily at them. There was music—faint, old, and familiar.

Nick blinked.

Gone.

But the warmth stayed.

"Thank you," Miranda said, her voice anchoring him back to now.

He met her gaze, steadier this time. "You're welcome."

44

Miranda sat at her desk, flipping through a few patient files, the mid-morning sunlight gently spilling through her office window. She had already seen several clients that morning, feeling a steady, reassuring rhythm settling back into place. Her mind was sharp, alert, and focused, but there was a subtle hum just beneath the surface—something she couldn't quite explain, a heightened intuition that felt more present than ever.

She had just finished making notes for an afternoon appointment when a soft knock sounded on her door.

"Come in, Lydia," Miranda called, a small smile tugging at the corner of her mouth.

The door opened gently, Lydia's curious expression appearing in the gap. "How'd you know it was me?"

Miranda set down her pen, leaning back in her chair with a faint smirk. "You're literally one of two people who ignore my 'Do not Disturb' sign. The other just happens to be off today."

Lydia grinned as she stepped into the office, quietly shutting the door behind her. Her playful demeanor shifted slightly as she approached Miranda's desk. "So, Carol just got a weird call at reception."

Miranda's brows knitted together in mild confusion. "What kind of weird call?"

Lydia crossed her arms, her tone more cautious now. "Some guy called asking specifically if you were here today. Didn't leave his name. When Carol confirmed you were in, he immediately hung up."

A subtle unease fluttered through Miranda's chest, but she kept her voice calm. "Did Carol say anything else about the call?"

"Just that he was polite but sounded... off," Lydia said softly. "Thought you should know."

Miranda nodded thoughtfully, taking a deep breath to steady the slight unease. "Thanks, Lydia."

"Of course," Lydia replied, hesitating a brief moment before continuing. "You sure you're good?"

Miranda met her friend's gaze confidently. "I'm fine. Really."

Lydia seemed reassured, nodding firmly. "Okay. Just shout if you need anything."

"You know I will," Miranda promised.

Lydia slipped back out of the office, closing the door softly behind her.

Miranda waited until the footsteps faded. Then she stood and crossed to the window.

The street outside looked normal. A mother pushing a stroller. A man unloading boxes from a delivery van. Nothing strange. Nothing alarming.

And yet, something felt wrong.

Her hand drifted to her belly.

Miranda stared out the window a moment longer, then pulled the blinds halfway shut.

It wasn't long before another soft knock came, this one quicker, sharper. Miranda looked up, sensing urgency before Lydia even spoke.

"Miranda, we have a laboring mom coming in," Lydia announced quickly, her voice steady but serious. "Riley Sawyer. She said her contractions have intensified very suddenly, and she's feeling something unusual."

Miranda stood swiftly, a sudden and undeniable certainty washing over her before Riley even stepped through the clinic doors. The words **shoulder dystocia** pulsed clearly in her mind, unmistakable and insistent. "Prepare Exam Room Two, please. I'll be right there."

Lydia nodded sharply, already moving.

Riley arrived moments later, clearly uncomfortable and distressed, her breathing rapid. Miranda moved swiftly to her side, checking Riley's progress and vitals. The subtle hum inside her seemed to pulse more insistently, guiding her every decision.

"I'm going to have you call Dr. Patel to be on standby," Miranda said quietly to Lydia, who was already at her side. "I know it's her day off, but just in case."

Lydia didn't question, simply nodding and quickly exiting to make the call. Miranda returned her full attention to Riley, offering quiet reassurance and steady strength.

Miranda remained calm, her instincts heightened as Riley's breathing quickened, signaling another intense contraction, Riley clutched the edge of the bed, her face tight with concentration.

"Riley, you're doing wonderfully," Miranda said gently, placing a reassuring hand on the woman's shoulder. "Listen to your body. Breathe down to your baby."

Riley nodded shakily, eyes squeezed shut. "It feels different this time—like pressure, but stuck somehow."

Miranda glanced briefly toward Grace, the young nurse assisting her today, sensing her quiet readiness.

"Riley, we're going to help you change positions," Miranda said confidently, guiding Riley gently yet firmly. "Let's bring your knees toward your chest, just like this. Grace, can you help her?"

"Of course," Grace answered promptly, stepping forward to help Miranda gently reposition Riley. Miranda remained calm, voice soothing but authoritative.

"Good. Right there. Now, with your next contraction, Riley, I want you to breathe steadily and give me a slow, controlled push. We've got this."

Riley met Miranda's eyes, finding reassurance in the steadiness she saw there. As the next contraction surged, Riley followed Miranda's gentle instruction, pushing carefully, guided entirely by the midwife's sure and steady hands.

Miranda felt the subtle release as the baby's shoulder slipped smoothly past the pubic bone, the tension dissolving instantly. She allowed herself a quiet breath of relief as the baby emerged easily into her waiting hands.

"There you go," Miranda whispered warmly, lifting the small, wriggling infant to Riley's chest. "You did it, Riley. Your baby is here."

Riley let out a relieved sob, tears streaming down her face as she embraced her newborn.

"You did amazing," Miranda praised softly, briefly meeting Grace's relieved gaze as the nurse discreetly nodded her silent approval.

Miranda's heart warmed, her hand resting momentarily on her own stomach. She couldn't explain exactly how she knew what was needed in that crucial moment—but she felt a quiet, comforting sense of peace that something beyond herself had helped guide her hands.

Wyatt stood at the edge of the parking lot, tucked behind a tree, jacket collar turned up against the chill, blending into the overcast afternoon. The hum of passing cars barely touched his ears; his attention was fixed entirely on the Fir Hollow Birth and Wellness clinic.

He'd waited there so long he nearly convinced himself to leave—to regroup and rethink—when the clinic door swung open.

Lydia stepped outside, phone pressed firmly to her ear. The door shut behind her with a gentle click.

Wyatt held his breath, stepping slightly deeper into the shadows, watching carefully as Lydia paced near the entrance.

"Hey, just wanted to give you a quick update—Riley's baby girl is here. Healthy and perfect, and Miranda handled it like the seasoned pro she is."

She paused, listening to the voice on the other end. "Yeah, she's alright. Tired, but what pregnant woman isn't?"

Wyatt froze.

Lydia kept talking, completely unaware. "I made her sit down for five minutes, but you know Miranda. She's already back at her desk like nothing happened."

She laughed quietly, then lowered her voice just a bit. "You were right though... the pregnancy's starting to wear on her. Not that she'd admit it."

Another beat of silence, and then: "Yes. I'm watching her. Always. Go enjoy your day off—I've got this."

She ended the call, slid her phone into her coat pocket, and turned back toward the building.

Wyatt didn't move.

Pregnant.

This wasn't just some curiosity anymore. It was confirmation. Proof.

And a new weakness.

A slow, calculating smile pulled at the corners of his mouth.

The lights were off in her office, save for the faint glow of the salt lamp on her desk. Miranda lay curled on the couch, one hand resting lightly over her belly.

The clinic had quieted again, the rush of adrenaline from earlier fading like a storm slipping off the horizon. Riley was fine. The baby was fine. Everything had turned out okay.

But she'd known. Before Riley ever walked through the door, she'd felt it—the way the tension had gathered behind her ribs like a warning.

And she had been right.

She pressed her palm a little firmer to her stomach, not expecting much—just hoping.

And then, there it was.

The faintest brush. Like the whisper of wings just beneath her skin.

Miranda froze, breath catching.

It wasn't strong. Barely noticeable, really. But it was real.

A flutter.

Tears priced at the corners of her eyes as she stayed perfectly still, her hand never moving.

"Hi, little one," she whispered. "I feel you. Are you the one helping me?"

She closed her eyes, a quiet ache blooming in her chest—for answers, for peace, for time to understand everything changing within her.

45

That night felt different.

Not colder, not louder—just... off. Like something had shifted a fraction to the left and left the world tilted. Miranda couldn't sleep. She hadn't even tried. There was a pressure in her chest that she couldn't explain, like the baby was holding its breath and waiting.

She sat at the old desk near the bedroom window, wrapped in one of Nick's flannels, a cup of untouched tea cooling at her side. Tinsel lay at her feet, eyes half-closed, but not sleeping. Watching.

Miranda placed a hand on her belly, rubbing gentle circles. "You feel it too, don't you?" she whispered. "Something's coming..."

The baby stirred. Just once. As if to say: yes.

Miranda exhaled and pulled a piece of paper from the drawer. Her hand hovered over the pen before she finally began to write.

She didn't know how long she wrote.

When she finally set the pen down, her eyes burned and her tea had long gone cold.

She folded the paper carefully, kissed it once, and slid it between the pages of her journal. Then she tucked the journal into the drawer, closed it softly, and pressed a hand over her heart.

"Just in case."

She looked down at her belly again, and the baby kicked gently, like a promise.

<h1 style="text-align:center">46</h1>

The house had settled into that kind of silence that only came after snowfall. Heavy. Still. Sacred.

Nick stood in the doorway of their bedroom, his shoulders outlined in soft firelight. Miranda was already inside, sitting at the edge of the bed in one of his old flannel shirts, legs tucked beneath her, hands resting on her belly.

She looked up at him.

"You're staring," she murmured.

"I'm trying to memorize you," he said, his voice rough and quiet. "Every freckle. Every breath."

Her smile was faint, a little sad. "You used to say that before."

"I did?"

Miranda nodded, patting the space beside her. "Before the accident. When you'd come in covered in sawdust and snow and still make time to dance with me in the kitchen."

Nick walked slowly to her, sat down, but didn't touch her right away. His eyes searched her face like he was afraid to blink.

"I hate that I forgot," he admitted. "I hate that I've made you carry all of this alone."

"You didn't mean to." She reached over, took his hand. "You came back to me the moment you woke up and looked at me like I was the only person in the world. You don't have to remember to love someone, Nick. You just have to choose them."

He exhaled, slow and deliberate, like he'd been carrying it for weeks.

"I've been falling in love with you again every day," he said. "Even when I didn't understand why. You'd laugh or brush your hair behind your ear or say something sarcastic to Lydia, and I'd feel it like deja vu. Like part of me knew you."

Miranda leaned her head on his shoulder. "Maybe that part never left."

They sat like that for a while — not speaking, just listening to the sound of the fire cracking softly and the rhythm of their shared heartbeat.

Nick finally turned toward her, cupping her face gently.

"I want to remember everything," he whispered. "All of it. Us. The life we've built. The magic I know we have."

"You will," she said. "Or maybe... you already are."

She reached up, kissed him softly. Not urgent. Not hungry. Just true.

And then—Miranda pulled back, blinking in surprise.

"Oh," she breathed.

Nick's brow furrowed. "What?"

She took his hand, placed it over her belly. "The baby just kicked."

He stilled completely.

A second later, it happened again—a firm little thump beneath his palm.

His eyes widened, breath catching in his throat as emotion rose fast and hard.

"I felt it," he said, voice thick. "I can't believe I—" He broke off, overwhelmed.

Miranda nodded, tears already slipping down her cheeks. "The baby wanted you to know. You're here. You're theirs."

And then he kissed her again—but this time it was everything.

The past. The future. The pieces of himself he hadn't even realized were missing—falling back into place, one by one.

Miranda knew it the moment he kissed her again: they had found their way back to each other.

They came together like the world had been holding its breath for this—waiting, watching.

And afterward, wrapped in the hush of the night and the warmth of each other, their breathing slowed.

Until Nick's body stilled.

He sat up slightly, blinking. His chest rose sharply as if something had slammed into him —not physically, but from the inside out.

"Nick?" Miranda sat up with him, touching his arm. "What is it?"

He turned to her slowly, eyes wide, filling with tears.

"I remember," he breathed. "Miranda... I remember everything."

Nick's hand drifted to her belly, resting over the gentle curve. His touch was tender. Reverent.

Miranda held him tighter, her heart thudding against his. The man she loved—the real Nick—was finally back.

But something in the air still felt...off.

Of course, she realized, we're still off-season. Even with his memories restored, the magic can't reach its full strength unless we're home.

His eyes shimmered with love, but beneath the surface, she could still sense it: the flickering weight of magic that hadn't yet fully returned.

They weren't whole—not yet. But they would be.

For a moment, he said nothing—just looked at her, like he was seeing her all over again.

Then, quietly:

"You're really showing now."

There was wonder in every syllable.

"I missed it... the beginning. I missed watching you become this."

Miranda brushed her fingers over the back of his hand.

"It's okay," she said softly. "You're seeing it now."

Miranda looked down at his hand, then back up at him—and this time, she didn't hold back.

Her eyes sparkled with tears, but they weren't just from relief. They were from joy.

"You remember everything," she whispered, voice shaking with emotion. "Nick... *you remember.*"

He nodded, his own throat too thick to speak.

And then she laughed—a bright, breathless sound like sunlight breaking through the snow. She cupped his face, kissed him over and over, her hands cradling his jaw like she couldn't believe he was real.

"You remember," she whispered again, forehead pressed to his. "All of it. Us. The bakery. The sleigh. The snow angel you made in your flannel pajamas because you lost a bet. Giving Dasher crap for being mean to Vixen."

He let out a choked laugh. "You made me wear the elf hat for a week."

She beamed, tears still falling. "I don't even care. I'd make you wear it forever if it meant this."

Nick kissed her like a promise, like an apology, like he'd never forget again.

When they finally settled into each other, his hand found its way back to her belly.

"She's really in there," he murmured, voice breaking.

Miranda smiled through her tears. "Or he."

He blinked. "Oh no. It's a she. I can feel it. She's going to have your eyes and your fire and your habit of leaving cookie dough on every surface in the kitchen."

Miranda giggled, tucking herself closer. "And your stubbornness. Your heart."

Their fingers intertwined across her stomach.

They fell asleep wrapped in each other, the quilt pulled high and the room aglow with the soft hush of a world at rest.

For the first time in a long while, there were no walls between them.

No forgotten memories.

No aching silences.

Just love—steady, warm, and whole.

Miranda lay still, her hand resting lightly over his, both of them curved protectively over her belly. Nick's breathing had evened out, slow and steady.

Her heart ached with the weight of everything they'd walked through to get back to this moment.

Thank you, she whispered in her mind, a stray tear falling down her cheek. *For not letting go of us when I wanted to give up. For bringing him back. For this.*

She didn't need words or signs.

This—Nick's arm around her, the baby safe inside her, the stillness after the storm—was enough.

Morning came with golden light slipping through the curtains.

Miranda woke first, slipping quietly out of bed to get ready for the day. She didn't want to leave, not really, but part of her longed for routine—for normalcy, even just for a few hours. The baby gave a soft kick as she stood in front of the mirror, and she smiled, resting a hand over the growing curve.

Nick stirred as she finished getting dressed. He reached for her sleepily, and when his hand found empty space, his eyes opened.

"I'll be at the clinic," she whispered, leaning over to kiss his forehead. "You rest."

He caught her hand before she pulled away, laced their fingers together. "Not today. I've got something I need to make."

She raised an eyebrow, but he only smiled—that old smile, the one that reached his eyes.

"A surprise?" she asked.

He kissed her hand. "A love letter. In wood."

Miranda's heart squeezed.

They didn't say anything more.

She left with a quiet heart and soft steps, and he rose a few minutes later, heading out to the shop with purpose in his stride and something warm humming under his skin—magic, maybe.

The kind that only wakes up when love is remembered.

47

The back door gave with a soft click.

No lock. No alarm. No resistance.

Wyatt slipped inside like a breath of cold air, closing the door behind him without a sound. He didn't need to hurry. He'd been watching long enough to know their routines.

Miranda was at the clinic.

Nick was in the shop.

The cat—the strange one—was with him.

It was the perfect window.

He moved through the house like someone who'd been there before. Careful, measured.

He didn't touch the photos on the wall, didn't disturb the worn throw blanket on the couch or the mug beside the sink. He wasn't here to destroy.

He was here for proof.

Up the stairs. Down the hall. The bedroom door creaked softly on its hinges, but no one heard. He stood in the doorway for a moment, taking it in—the flannel shirt draped over the chair, the faint scent of lavender lingering in the air.

Her world. Her life. Frozen in the middle of an ordinary day.

He crossed to the nightstand and opened the drawer.

There were pens, a half-used journal, a folded letter he didn't read—and beneath that... the photo.

A single black and white image, grainy and ghostlike, but unmistakable.

An ultrasound.

His breath caught.

It was real.

He held the photo in shaking fingers, eyes narrowing as his mind spun with questions he hadn't dared ask before. How long had she been pregnant? What kind of a child could come from her?

He slipped the photo into the envelope with the others. The final piece. The one that made the third box complete.

He didn't linger. He'd been there too long already.

Down the stairs. Out the door. Gone.

The clinic smelled faintly of peppermint and freshly brewed coffee—a comfort she hadn't noticed until today.

Miranda moved through the morning with a lightness in her step, one hand instinctively resting on her belly as she greeted patients, checked charts, and let Lydia make entirely too many jokes about her glowing "new mom energy."

She didn't care. Let them tease.

Nick remembered.

Every smile he'd ever given her. Every kiss in the snow. Every late-night cookie disaster and whispered promise—he remembered it all.

For the first time in months, she felt whole again.

By the time her last appointment wrapped up and the waiting room emptied, she floated into her office and barely had the door closed before—

"Okay. Spill."

Dr. Anaya Patel leaned against the desk with her arms crossed, one eyebrow already raised and clearly ready for battle.

Miranda blinked. "Spill what?"

"You're humming," Anaya said, eyes narrowing. "You don't hum. You barely tolerate humming. Something happened. Spill."

Miranda laughed, warmth blooming across her face. "You're ridiculous."

"You're radiant. Like you've just come back from a private retreat on a magical glacier and found enlightenment."

Miranda opened her mouth.

Anaya pointed at her. "Don't say it's hormones."

"It's not," Miranda admitted, cheeks flushed.

Anaya's eyes sparkled. "So?"

"So... he remembers," Miranda said softly.

There was a beat of silence before Anaya straightened, eyes widening. "Wait. All of it?"

Miranda nodded, eyes misting as she smiled. "Everything."

Anaya just stared at her for a second—then broke into a huge grin. "Oh. Oh wow. No wonder you're walking around here like a Christmas movie commercial."

Miranda rolled her eyes, but the laughter bubbled up before she could stop it.

Anaya sobered a little. "You okay?"

"I'm better than okay." Miranda placed a hand on her belly. "For the first time in a long time... I feel like we're finally back."

Anaya didn't say anything for a moment—just nodded and gave Miranda's hand a small squeeze.

"Good," she said quietly. "You deserve this."

Anaya perched on the corner of Miranda's desk like she owned the place—which, Miranda had to admit, she kind of did on personality alone.

"So when did it happen?" Anaya asked, already in full investigator mode. "Did he just wake up and go, 'Ah yes, flannel and sleigh bells—it's all coming back to me now?' or was it more dramatic?"

Miranda laughed again. "Not dramatic. Just... real. We were talking, and then we weren't talking. And after—" she hesitated, cheeks pinking.

Anaya raised an eyebrow. "After, huh?"

Miranda shot her a look. "Not going into detail."

"Rude," Anaya muttered, smirking. "I live for this."

"But afterward," Miranda said softly, her hand drifting to her belly again, "he looked at me and he just... knew. He remembered. He said my name like it meant something again."

Anaya's smirk melted into something softer, more reverent. "That's kind of beautiful."

Miranda nodded, blinking past the sudden sting in her eyes. "It was."

Anaya tapped her foot. "Okay, last question—for now."

"I'm afraid."

"You should be." She grinned. "How's it feel... knowing this little one is coming into a world where their dad knows again? Where everything that matters is finally in place?"

Miranda paused, her heart fluttering.

"It feels like..." She looked down at her belly, the baby shifting gently beneath her hand. "Like we're standing at the very beginning of something beautiful."

Anaya tilted her head. "Then let it stay beautiful, okay?"

Miranda looked up. "What do you mean?"

"Just a feeling." Anaya offered a half-shrug, then tempered it with a smile. "You know me. Science brain. Gut instincts. Both are twitchy today."

Miranda tried to laugh it off. "You and Lydia, I swear..."

But something cold brushed the edge of her thoughts.

Just a flicker.

Just a shadow.

She shook it off and stood. "I'm going to finish charting before I start leaking feelings all over the paperwork."

Anaya rolled her eyes but stood too. "Fine. But if you name this baby something boring like John or Carol after all this drama, I'm protesting the birth certificate."

"I'll take that under advisement," Miranda called as she opened the office door—still smiling, but her chest just a little tighter than before.

48

The scent of cedar lingered thick in the air, mingling with sawdust and the faint, comforting creak of old floorboards beneath Nick's boots.

He was humming.

Not a song he recognized—just something low and warm that had found its way out of his chest without asking. The kind of sound you make when your world finally fits back together.

Tinsel lay curled nearby on a folded blanket, her golden eyes half-lidded as she watched the shavings curl away from his chisel. Every so often, her tail flicked. She wasn't quite asleep, but she wasn't uneasy either. Just... watching.

Nick leaned over the workbench, focused and steady. The smooth curve of wood was taking shape beneath his hands—the beginnings of a rocking chair. Not just any chair. Her chair. For nights when the baby wouldn't sleep, for the quiet moments when she'd need somewhere to just be.

He smiled to himself, smoothing the next pass of the chisel.

"She's gonna say it's too much," he muttered softly, glancing at Tinsel. "Then she'll sit in it for ten minutes and refuse to get up."

Tinsel blinked like she agreed.

Nick paused, running a hand through his hair, now dusted with fine wood particles. He set the tool down for a second and let his fingers trail over the carved pattern on the backrest—a simple, swirling design that reminded him of snowflakes and wind and her laugh when she caught snow on her tongue.

He rested his hand on the curve of the seat, eyes softening.

"I'm gonna give you everything I've got," he whispered—not to the chair, but to the child he hadn't met yet. "Every ounce of love I almost forgot."

The shop was quiet except for the wind stirring gently outside. Nick took a deep breath and picked up his chisel again.

49

The sky had shifted by the time Miranda pulled into the driveway—streaks of gray rolling in over the trees, soft and low. The kind of clouds that made you want to light a candle and pull a blanket close.

She smiled anyway.

Everything still felt new—like the world had been washed clean overnight.

Nick had remembered everything just last night, and it was still sinking in.

Every time he looked at her, she swore she could see whole lifetimes behind his eyes.

They hadn't stopped smiling since.

Her day at the clinic had been calm. Simple. Lydia was in a good mood, which usually meant trouble, and Anaya had only asked four hundred and twelve questions instead of her usual thousand. Miranda had made it to the afternoon without crying or snapping, which felt like a victory.

And now, she just wanted to go home—to tell Nick about the baby names she and Lydia had joked about. To hear him laugh. To maybe sneak into the woodshop and see what he was making—the so-called "love letter in wood" he wouldn't explain.

She walked up the steps, heart light.

And then she saw it.

A small cardboard box. Ordinary. Brown. No return address.

Placed neatly against the front door like it belonged there.

Her smile disappeared.

The warmth in her chest twisted. Her breath caught.

Not again.

She stood frozen for a beat too long, then bent down slowly and picked it up. It was light. Familiar in a way she had grown to dread. She carried it inside, closing the door softly behind her.

She didn't call for Nick. She didn't want him to see her like this—not yet.

At the kitchen table, she opened the box.

Three photos sat inside.

The first: a black and white image. Miranda and Arthur. Her hair pinned up, her smile soft. Another decade. Another lifetime.

The second: a newer photo. Mid-century. Her dress dated but elegant, her features unchanged.

The third: taken from the woods—of her, just that morning. She was locking the front door. She remembered the exact braid she'd worn, the coat she'd buttoned. Someone had been watching.

She nearly closed the box right then. Her hands were trembling. Her stomach turned.

But something caught her eye—tucked just beneath the others.

A fourth photo.

Not a portrait. Not a candid.

An ultrasound.

Her ultrasound.

She hadn't shown it to anyone but Nick.

She hadn't even taken it out of the nightstand drawer.

Her fingers clutched the edge of the table to keep from falling.

Someone had been in their house.

She dropped the photo like it burned her, hands flying to her mouth as her stomach turned in slow, rolling waves of disbelief.

It had been in the drawer. She'd put it there herself.

She stumbled back from the table, knocking the chair askew. Her mind screamed at her to stay calm, to think, to move, but her body wouldn't obey.

It wasn't just being watched anymore.

It wasn't just being followed.

Whoever had taken that photo had been inside. *Inside their home.*

Who is doing this? What do they want?

She grabbed the box, dumped the contents back in, and ran to the stairs—two at a time. She nearly tripped turning into the bedroom, fumbling for the drawer, already knowing what she wouldn't find.

The envelope was gone. The photo was gone.

She pressed both hands against the edge of the dresser, trying to breathe. The baby shifted slightly—a soft nudge beneath her ribs—and she swore she felt something deeper than movement.

A warning.

She closed her eyes. "I know," she whispered. "I know."

The sound of the back door creaked faintly downstairs.

Miranda froze.

Her eyes flew open. She reached for her phone, but it wasn't in her pocket. It wasn't on the nightstand.

Footsteps moved softly below.

Slow. Intentional.

She turned toward the window—thought about calling for Nick—but the baby rolled again, harder this time, and her instinct screamed.

She wasn't supposed to shout.

She wasn't supposed to move.

She was supposed to listen.

Then she heard it—her name. Spoken low. Familiar.

Her body trembled, knees threatening to give out. She pressed a hand over her belly, eyes scanning the room like the walls might open and swallow her whole.

God, please...

The prayer wasn't elegant. It wasn't even fully formed. But it was real.

Protect us. Show me what to do.

Her pulse pounded in her ears as she backed away from the dresser, heart hammering in rhythm with her fear.

The voice came again.

"Miranda."

She didn't recognize the voice.

But it knew her.

"Miranda."

She took a step back from the dresser, her heart hammering against her ribs. The voice wasn't loud. It wasn't harsh. It was quiet—almost gentle.

That made it worse.

She turned slowly, her body shielding her stomach on instinct.

And there he was.

Standing in the doorway, like he belonged there.

Mid-thirties. Blond hair. Calm eyes that didn't match the tension in the room.

He smiled like an old friend.

"I've been wondering how long it would take you to figure it out."

Miranda didn't speak. Her throat had closed up, and the baby had gone still, as if waiting.

The man took a step into the room

"You haven't aged. Not a day. Just like the pictures."

Her legs were shaking, but she forced herself to stay upright.

"You're Arthur's grandson," she said, voice flat.

His smile twitched. "So you do remember him."

"I remember everything."

He nodded like he expected the answer.

"I didn't come to hurt you," he said. "I just want the truth."

Miranda's eyes flicked toward the door. Could she run? Could she scream loud enough?

But he saw it. Read it in her face.

"Don't," he said softly. "Please don't."

And before she could move, before she could shout for Nick, he stepped forward.

Everything blurred. Her body reacted, but she wasn't fast enough.

His hand closed around her arm—not rough, but firm—and then the room spun.

Outside, the wind picked up. Tinsel lifted her head suddenly in the woodshop, her fur standing on end. A soundless growl rumbled in her throat.

Nick didn't notice.

He was smoothing the final edge of the rocker, humming softly.

50

Nick wiped his hands on an old rag, brushing sawdust from his jeans as he stepped out of the shop.

The air had cooled. Clouds pressed low against the treetops, and a hush had settled over the property—not peaceful exactly. Expectant.

He glanced toward the house, smiling without thinking.

She'd be home by now. He'd surprise her with the rocker tomorrow, maybe—or pretend to be grumpy that she tried to sneak a peak.

He stepped onto the porch, boots thudding softly against the wood.

"Red?" he called, pushing open the front door.

Silence.

He stepped inside. The lights were still off. Her coat wasn't on the hook. Her bag wasn't by the table.

"Miranda?" Louder this time.

No answer.

A strangle prickle crawled across the back of his neck. Tinsel darted past his leg and into the house, tail low, moving faster than usual. She didn't stop—just ran straight for the stairs, claws skittering against the wood.

"Tinsel—?" He followed her instinctively, pulse beginning to race.

The kitchen smelled wrong. Not like her.

He turned and saw the box.

Nick crossed the room in two steps, heart slamming against his ribs as he looked inside. He didn't need to pick them up. He already knew.

He recognized the ultrasound.

He recognized the handwriting on the envelope he'd seen her tuck into the drawer.

And then he saw the chair.

Not tucked in. Not where she would've left it.

Knocked over.

His breath caught.

"Miranda?!" He yelled as he turned and bolted up the stairs.

Bedroom: empty.

Bathroom: empty.

He ran from room to room, calling her name, louder and louder, voice cracking.

"Tinsel!" he shouted. "Find her!"

The cat was already moving—frantically now, darting from room to room, tail fluffed, her breath hissing in quick bursts.

Nick stumbled back to the kitchen, grabbed his phone with shaking hands.

No message. No call. No clue.

Only the box.

Only the silence.

Only the awful, clawing truth that the woman he had just gotten back—the woman carrying his child—was gone.

Letter to Heaven

Dear Aunt Cindylou,

There's not a day that goes by that I don't miss you with all my heart. Every dream with you in it feels like a gentle reminder—like you're reawakening my memories and whispering, *I'm still here.* It still physically hurts knowing I can't talk to you anymore. But you gave me something I didn't even realize I had until recently: a deep love for storytelling. Because of you, I've started writing books that I truly want to share—with joy, with faith, and sometimes just enough chaos to make someone say, *what the heck just happened?* In your memory, I'm dedicating every book I write to the original Story Princess—**you.** From your Story Princess 2.0, I promise your storytelling will live on through me. And I can't wait to see where this road takes me. Please tell everyone in heaven I said hello... and that I miss every single one of you dearly.

Love always,

Hannah

About the Author

Hannah Hunt is a storyteller, a dreamer, and a firm believer in quiet magic. She's been writing stories in her head for as long as she can remember—but it wasn't until *Frosted Secrets* that she finally found the courage to put one on paper.

When she's not writing, Hannah is a devoted wife, a proud mother to a wildly imaginative toddler, and a lifelong lover of all things cozy and whimsical. She draws inspiration from long talks with her grandmother and the legacy of her Aunt Cindylou—the original Story Princess in her life.

She also enjoys playing video games with her husband—as long as her toddler doesn't need her attention, of course.

Hannah lives in Illinois and shares bookish joy, behind-the-scenes updates, and Story Princess magic on Instagram at @storyprincess2.0.

Frosted Secrets is her debut novel and the first in the Frosted Series.

Acknowledgement

Writing this book has been one of the hardest and most fulfilling things I've ever done—and I didn't do it alone.

To my family: thank you for loving me through the chaos. Your patience, encouragement, and late-night hugs mean more than you know.

To my best friend, who cheered me on through every high and low—you reminded me that my voice matters. Thank you for always believing I'd finish this, even when I didn't.

To the people who listened to me talk about this book non-stop(yes, you, coworkers), thank you for nodding along like you weren't secretly planning your escape. I owe you coffee. Probably several.

To the readers—thank you for picking up this book and giving it a piece of your time. I hope you find something meaningful in these pages.

This story lived in my head long before I ever wrote a single word. It stayed with me—quiet, persistent, patient—waiting for the moment I was ready to bring it to life. If you're reading this book now, that means I finally did. And that still feels unreal.

To anyone out there wondering if they could write a book: You can. Start messy. Keep going. Let your story take root and grow.